CW01663660

MAUGHAM'

The stories are often shocking, even violent, and their ingredients are sexual jealousy, hatred, revenge, cowardice, failure. They are frank, and the manner of their telling is naked and plain, without flowers or frills or ornaments. In other words, they are in that naturalistic tradition which began with Guy de Maupassant: they depict life just as the author met it. But there is compassion, and often there is humour. Men and women are weak creatures, as Maugham well knew, but it is not up to either author or reader to condemn them for their weakness. Judgement is for God, if there is a God (so Maugham seems to say); the great human virtue is tolerance.

Maugham's MALAYSIAN *Stories*

Selected and with an Introduction by

Anthony Burgess

MANDARIN

A Mandarin Paperback

MAUGHAM'S MALAYSIAN STORIES

First published 1969
by Heinemann Educational Books (Asia) Ltd
Reprinted 1975, 1978, 1982, 1984, 1988, 1989
This edition published 1994
by Mandarin Paperbacks
a division of Reed International (Singapore) Pte Ltd
Consumer/Education Books
37 Jalan Pemimpin #07-04/05, Block B
Union Industrial Building, Singapore 2057

Mandarin is an imprint of Reed Consumer Books Ltd

ISBN 9971 64 165 8

Cover design by Kowling
Cover photo: Courtesy of Tourism
Development Corporation of Malaysia

Printed in Singapore
by Kin Keong Printing Co. Pte. Ltd.

Contents

Introduction

William Somerset Maugham died in 1965, at the great age of ninety-one. His life was not only long but industrious. While still a young medical student in London, he achieved success with a novel called *Liza of Lambeth*, which is still read and has even been turned into a television play. From youth till old age he maintained a steady output of novels, plays, short stories, travel-books, and works which may be termed contemplative and critical. His writings made him a very rich man and, for many years after his death, they are likely to go on earning handsome royalties. There is a tendency among lovers of literature to doubt the literary merit of books that make their author wealthy. If a book is very popular, it is argued, it must have been written to appeal to uncultivated minds (which, of course, are commoner than cultivated ones), and therefore there must be something coarse, obvious, superficial about a popular book. Sometimes this is true, but not always. There are important writers – like Henry James – who have never had a very wide appeal. On the other hand, writers like Charles Dickens have combined great popularity with the highest literary excellence. Somerset Maugham's excellence is not of the highest, but it is high enough. His achievements in the field of the novel cannot compare with those of either Dickens or James, but he wrote at least two great novels, and in the minor form of the short story there are very few writers – living or dead – to touch him.

Maugham was one of the first British writers of fiction to present aspects of life which had, for a long time, been considered unmentionable in literature. Read Dickens and, though you will find a certain amount of violence (in *Oliver Twist*, for instance), you will never find any frank mention of sex. In nineteenth-century British fiction, there was a taboo on the depiction of what twentieth-century novelists take in their stride – not only the sexual act, but the human body itself. Romantic love was permissible, but not raw lust. The less savoury aspects of physical life – excretion, disease and wounds – were more or less fumigated out of existence. In France, there was less squeamishness. Gustave Flaubert, about the middle of the nineteenth century, was almost clinically honest in *Madame Bovary*. Towards the end of the century, Emile Zola in his novels and Guy de Maupassant in his short stories seemed not merely clinically but brutally honest.

The cult of *naturalism*, as it was called, shocked those British novel-readers who came into contact with it. Zola and Maupassant were condemned as "dirty", immoral, and cynical when, in fact, they were doing no more than reminding the reading public that life is not all honour, virtue, duty and pretty flowers. Life can be noble, but it can also be sordid, and it is the task of the honest writer to show the whole of life. And so fornication, adultery, the smell of meat markets, physical cruelty, idiocy, exactly rendered death all made their appearance in the Zolaesque novel and the Maupassant-type short story. Moderate readers complained, perhaps with justice, that these aspects of the real world were not balanced by the traditional ones: there was plenty that was physical, but hardly anything of the spiritual at all. As for language – where was the old beauty, poetry, uplift? In Maupassant especially the style was clipped, economical, matter-of-fact, dry. And humour was no longer a matter of grotesque rough-and-tumble and belly-laughs. It was subtle and ironical, and sometimes cruel.

Somerset Maugham's short stories are the nearest thing we have in English to the *contes* of Maupassant. That he could write dry, plain, ironic studies of human life which, we think, come most naturally to the French temperament, may be accounted to various circumstances, but we have to note that Maugham was born and brought up in France. Paris was the first city he knew, and when, at the age of ten, he first set foot in England, the first words he uttered were "*Porteur! Cabriolet!*" ("Porter! Cab!"). French was as much his language as English, and it gave him an *entrée* into a literature that was not very well known in England at the beginning of the present century. He was able to get at the new French fiction-writers direct, and not through belated and often poor translations.

But (granted a writing talent) a childhood spent in Paris and an ability to read French literature with ease are not enough to turn a potential author into a sort of English Maupassant. We have to consider what sort of man Somerset Maugham was, or rather what sort of boy. In the first place, he had a physical disability which made him stand outside the world as an observer, instead of – like Charles Dickens – engaging the world joyously and robustly. He stammered, and the stammer was agony to him. To his nephew Robin Maugham he recounted bitter stories of the humiliation that stammer caused him as a boy. As for instance when he tried to buy a railway ticket to Whitstable and, at the station ticket office, could not get the word out. "I just stood there stammering. People behind me were getting impatient, but I still couldn't say 'Whitstable'. Suddenly two men stepped out of the queue and pushed me aside. 'We can't wait all night for you,' they said; 'stop wasting our time.' So I had to go to the back of the queue and start all over again." And there were the humiliations of the classroom, where inability to get a word out was regarded as a symptom of stupidity. It is no wonder that the young Willie Somerset Maugham was a shy and bitter watcher of the world, rather than an active participant in its work and fun.

Not that, in his youth in that same Whitstable, where he lived with his clergyman uncle, he had much opportunity for fun. Life was depressing and restricted, and it was further saddened by the death of his mother, whom he adored, and by the discovery that his family – which he had always believed to be distinguished and rich – was in fact poor and of little account. His life was to be devoted to regilding the family name and to making money, but the early near-poverty in a dull and repressive home left its mark. In later life, Maugham the successful was still capable of pessimism and even self-pity. He was not a happy man, though he had everything that money could buy, friends, good health and a large talent. He could look on life in a thin-lipped and cynical way, and many of his stories demonstrate how nasty people can be and how disappointment and disaster are always waiting to blot out the sunlight.

Maugham, then, had a natural tendency to pessimism; neither he nor his characters may be thought of as expecting too much out of life. But such good things as life offers must be relished to the full – music, for instance, and wine; curries and the French cuisine; the natural beauties of sea and land; the immense variety of the human race; a game of bridge and a whisky and soda. One must be wary, though, of expecting too much from people, as opposed to things. People swear eternal love to you, and then they let you down. And, Maugham always seems to imply, we must not expect too much from

God, either. For that matter, God probably does not exist: there is no heaven after death, and there is enough hell on earth. One must live life stoically, as the Romans did – enjoying the wine and the roses, accepting misfortune without complaining overmuch, awaiting without fear a death that will be "*una nox dormienda*" (a night to be slept through), or – as Sir Winston Churchill put it – an eternity of "black velvet".

Since he himself was capable of so much suffering, Maugham was quick to sympathize with the sufferings of others. He is not a Christian writer, but he is tolerant and even charitable. He condemns no wrongs: he merely records them without comment. The unpleasant characters in his novels and stories are the ones who think too much of themselves, or pretend to virtue when they are really just as vicious as the rest of us; for rogues, wanderers, misfits, failures there is kindness and something like love. His best novel, *Cakes and Ale*, gives us a fair demonstration of his sympathies and antipathies. It is the story of a great writer, Edward Driffield, and his wife Rosie. Rosie is unfaithful, giving herself freely to any man who wants her, and eventually she leaves her husband to go off with a coal merchant. A moral writer, a writer in the Christian tradition, would condemn such a woman, but Maugham evidently feels nothing but affection for her. At least she is honest with herself; she does not pretend to be something she is not. The characters we are intended to dislike are ambitious people, people who think highly of themselves, sanctimonious people, hypocrites, snobs. One such character in *Cakes and Ale* is the novelist Alroy Kear, who was based on a real-life novelist, Hugh Walpole (Walpole recognized himself in the book and was, understandably, very hurt). Maugham's weapon of demolition is not scorn but humour. Walpole is long dead, but generations to come will go on laughing at Alroy Kear: he sums up so many of the faults of the pompously successful.

It is not really strange that a pessimistic writer should also be a humorous writer. Maugham, as a young man, had sufferings of his own and, as a medical student helping to deliver babies in London's poverty-stricken East End, he saw much of the sufferings of others. It has been said that, when one looks at the wrongs, injustices and agonies of the world, one can either laugh or cry: both bitter tears and bitter laughter are means of discharging anger and hopelessness. The bitter laughter, the ridicule, the mockery which is half-sympathetic – these all spring in Maugham not from a riotous sense of fun or a desire to be cruel but from a sense of the absurdity of human life. Life is absurd because of its divisions – the division between man's desires and man's limited capabilities; the division between those who have and those who have not; the division between beauty and ugliness; the division of the human make-up itself into the body that wars with the mind. A good deal of Maugham's humour is termed ironical. To take an example from *Cakes and Ale*: Rosie Driffield is married to a great and revered author, yet she runs off to America with a coal merchant. When, at the end of the book, she is asked why she chose to marry this latter man (now deceased), she answers: "Because he was always such a gentleman." Irony is the quality we see in contradiction; we expect one thing and we get another; we want a thing but are granted it when we no longer want it. Irony is the sinner really being a saint. It is also a man being crucified by the world because he wants to save the world.

Another fine novel of Maugham's – *The Moon and Sixpence* – is a prolonged study in irony. The hero is a banker who has everything any sane man could desire –

a good wife, children, a comfortable home, a sufficient fortune. But suddenly, in middle age, he announces that he is going to leave all this behind and become a painter. And so he does, embracing poverty and loneliness in Paris and, later, leprosy in Tahiti; he is driven by the demon of art. What looks like a failed life to the outside world is, of course, success on a different level of values. For this strange hero is based closely on the real-life painter Paul Gauguin who, if he had remained a comfortable man of business, would be forgotten today; as it is, he is regarded as one of the great geniuses of all time.

It is typical of Maugham that he should base a novel on a real person. *Cakes and Ale* is based on real figures from the world of literature, and *Of Human Bondage* – his longest novel – is a retelling of his own early life (though a limp is substituted for a stammer). Admittedly, all his books contain a good deal of invention, but his cult of naturalism, or realism, led him to portray the real world rather than an imaginary one. Life taught him, we must suppose, that no fiction could touch truth for strangeness, irony, shock. Why should he invent themes for stories when his own experience – as well as what he read in newspapers and biographies – could provide so many remarkable ones? Maugham's inventiveness lies on the surface – changed names, imagined conversations and so on; much of what he describes actually happened.

Knowing this, we may be tempted to assume that the narrator of so many of Maugham's novels and stories is Maugham himself. He prefers to tell his stories in the first person: they are mostly what children call "I-stories". But the "I" is not necessarily Maugham himself. Sometimes it is, but more often it is Maugham as he likes to imagine himself. In one novel, his last, *The Razor's Edge*, the "I" is obviously William Somerset

Maugham, and in the film of the book it is surprising to see William Somerset Maugham as one of the characters – played, however, not by himself but by a professional actor. But it would be wise of us to accept the "I" of most of his stories as an invention, a convenient device for making his narrative direct and immediate. If I want to tell a friend a ghost story, I can make it more horrible – because more credible – if I make myself the chief character in the tale. Maugham uses not only the "I" which seems to be the author himself but, whenever he can, first person narratives within the main first person narrative. *The Moon and Sixpence* is full of people telling their own stories about the painter Strickland: "I" after "I" after "I".

A good number of the stories in this volume are not, in fact, first person narratives, but the way the stories are told suggests a man sitting down with his friends after a game of bridge and, over glasses of whisky and soda, spinning a plain tale. Maugham's style of writing is a spoken style – easy, unforced, totally relaxed. It is, if you like, an "unliterary" style. Faced with the task of describing a Malayan sunset, a "literary" writer feels called upon to throw words about as a painter throws paint – "an apocalyptical accession of hushed luminosity, the reds and purples and ochres blasting like archangelic trumpets" – that sort of thing. Maugham is content to say: "The sun went down. I went to the club for a *stengah* and a game of billiards." When Graham Sutherland painted his portrait of Maugham, he gave him the appearance of an Oriental story-teller: a man *speaking* his tales, not laboriously setting them down with a pen.

I have said a little about Maugham the novelist, but here, of course, we are concerned with Maugham as a creator of some of the best short stories ever written.

The short story is his true medium and, indeed, even his best novel, *Cakes and Ale*, has the "feel" of a short story (it was, in fact, originally planned as a short story). *The Moon and Sixpence* reads like a number of separate short narratives, all about the same hero. His novel *Theatre* is a loose collection of episodes in the life of an actress – not a closely-knit single entity like one of the novels of Henry James. He is happiest with the short story: he knows it is the form he can manage best. And he wrote a great number of short stories.

In old age, having decided that it was unlikely that he would ever write any more, Maugham collected all the short stories he thought worth preserving in three large volumes. They are all what are known as "commercial" stories; they were written for magazines, often at the request of magazine editors, and their lengths depended on the number of words that editors thought they could use. Some are very short; others are like brief novels. He cut his cloth according to the magazine's measure. The range of these stories is very wide, especially as regards geographical location. While Maupassant set nearly all his stories in France, Maugham travelled the world in search of places to write about: foreign travel stimulated his story-telling faculty. There are very few countries he visited which did not yield at least one story, and some countries yielded many more than one.

What Maugham called his "Malayan" stories are not all about the territory which was once named the Federated Malay States and later the Federation of Malaya; they are not even confined to the bigger entity now called Malaysia. To Maugham, "Malaya" served to describe the former Dutch East Indies, and even certain Pacific areas, as well as the true Malayan territories. In those days of cheap travel which came after the First World War, Maugham spent a great deal of time voyaging from island to island, port to port, settlement to settlement. He stayed in no one place very long, but he usually managed to absorb something of the atmosphere of each town, village or rubber estate he visited, and he always made quick contact with the local residents. These residents were invariably Europeans – planters, colonial officials, businessmen, or just men living in exile to escape from trouble or sadness at home – and there is little evidence that Maugham gained, or wished to gain, any direct knowledge of the lives and customs of the native peoples of the East. This must be disappointing to present-day Malay and Indian and Chinese and Eurasian readers of his stories, but we have to remember that (apart from the fact that Maugham had no time to learn Malay or Chinese or Tamil) the Western attitude to the Far East was very different in Maugham's time from what it is today.

In the nineteen-twenties and 'thirties, the East Indian territories which were under Dutch and British rule or protection were not yet moving in the direction of independence. The newspapers of London and Amsterdam made no reference to politicians like Soekarno, Tunku Abdul Rahman and Lee Kuan Yew, since men of this kind had not yet made their appearance in Djakarta, Kuala Lumpur and Singapore. Sultans and rajas paid visits to Europe, but they were merely colourful Oriental figures; they were not associated with power or responsibility. When a European paid a visit to the East Indies, the only Malays, Indians and Chinese he would meet were coolies on the rubber estates, houseboys and cooks in bungalows, barmen in clubs and hotels, clerks in offices, orderlies in hospitals. He tended (especially if he could not speak their languages) to regard them as mere colourful "extras", with no opportunity to star in the drama of Oriental life. The forefront of the stage was monopolized by the men who ruled these territories – whether as Colonial Office civil servants or estate managers. A visitor like Maugham would talk and eat with these people (and their wives), and the Malays and Chinese would merely bring drinks and serve dinner. Maugham cannot be blamed for making his stories centre on these expatriate Europeans, since they were the only people he could really get to know. There are exceptions – the Malay woman in "P & O", for instance, and the Chinese clerk in "The Letter" – but these characters are not as fully drawn as the European characters who provide the substance of the story. If Maugham had started writing Malayan short stories in, say, 1954, his plots and main characters might have been very different.

You are to read, then, about a world long dead. And, as you will see from the Preface Maugham wrote for the third volume of his stories, the author himself became well aware of the changes that took place (between the writing of the stories and the collecting of them) in the lives of expatriate Europeans. But he did not become sufficiently aware of the changes that took place in the lives of the "natives" (a disparaging word in Maugham's day, and even in ours, though everybody in the world is a "native" of one place or another). Maugham belonged to an age in which the only people to be taken seriously in fiction were people of European stock. Still, Maugham's planters and officials remain very much alive as human beings, and we can be as much amused or moved by their tribulations today as Maugham's first readers were.

I said earlier that Maugham tended to base his stories on true events and real people. What I did not say is that this is a dangerous thing to do. If a person reads a story and recognizes himself as one of the characters, he may be hurt or angry, as Hugh Walpole was when he saw himself in Alroy Kear. And this hurt or anger may express itself in a libel action, whereby the person who recognizes himself in a story may take the author to court and try to gain substantial damages from him. Many of Maugham's Malayan stories are about real people (thinly disguised), and he was often in danger of libel actions. One of the most dangerous stories of all was "The Letter", which was based on a real crime committed in Singapore while Maugham was there, but there are plenty of other stories which got too near the horrid truth. On the whole, Maugham was lucky: he was never taken to court. But, till recently, there were ageing colonial expatriates who were angry and hurt and swore they would never forgive Maugham for placing them in his stories. But, as I said, the Maugham world is no longer with us, and we must read him not for scandal but for enjoyment.

The stories are often shocking, even violent, and their ingredients are sexual jealousy, hatred, revenge, cowardice, failure. They are frank, and the manner of their telling is naked and plain, without flowers or frills or ornaments. In other words, they are in that naturalistic tradition which began with Guy de Maupassant: they depict life just as the author met it. But there is compassion, and often there is humour. Men and women are weak creatures, as Maugham well knew, but it is not up to either author or reader to condemn them for their weakness. Judgement is for God, if there is a God (so Maugham seems to say); the great human virtue is tolerance.

A.B.

Preface

William Somerset Maugham had the following to say about his Malaysian stories:

They were written long before the Second World War and I should tell the reader that the sort of life with which they deal no longer exists. When I first visited those countries the lives the white men and their wives led there differed but little from what they had been twenty-five years before. They got home leave once in five years. They had besides a few weeks leave every year. If they lived where the climate was exhausting they sought the fresh air of some hill-station not too far away; if, like some of the government servants, they lived where they might not see another white man for weeks on end, they went to Singapore so that they might consort for a time with their kind. The Times when it arrived at a station upcountry, in Borneo for instance, was six weeks old and they were lucky if they received the Singapore paper in a fortnight.

Aviation has changed all that. Even before the war people who could afford it were able to spend even their short leave at home. Papers, illustrated weeklies, magazines reached them fresh from the press. In the old days Sarawak, say, or Selangor were where they expected to spend their lives till it was time for them to retire on a pension; England was very far away and when at long intervals they went back was increasingly strange to them; their real home, their intimate friends, were in the land in which the better part of their lives was spent. But with the rapidity of communication it remained an alien land, a temporary rather than a permanent habitation, which circumstances obliged them for a spell to occupy; it was a longish halt in a life that had its roots in the Sussex downs or on the moors of Yorkshire. Their ties with the homeland, which before had insensibly loosened and sometimes broke asunder, remained fast. England, so to speak, was round the corner. They no longer felt cut off. It changed their whole outlook.

The countries of which I wrote were then at peace. It may be that some of those peoples, Malays, Dyaks, Chinese, were restive under the British rule, but there was no outward sign of it. The British gave them justice, provided them with hospitals and schools, and encouraged their industries. There was no more crime than anywhere else. An unarmed man could wander through the length of the Federated Malay States in perfect safety. The only real trouble was the low price of rubber.

There is one more point I want to make. Most of these stories are on the tragic side. But the reader must not suppose that the incidents I have narrated were of common occurrence. The vast majority of these people, government servants, planters and traders, who spent their working lives in Malaya were ordinary people ordinarily satisfied with their station in life. They did the jobs they were paid to do more or less competently. They were as happy with their wives as are most married couples. They led humdrum lives and did very much the same things every day. Sometimes by way of a change they got a little shooting; but as a rule, after they had done their day's work, they played tennis if there were people to play with, went to the club at sundown if there was a club in the vicinity, drank in moderation and played bridge. They had their little tiffs, their little jealousies, their little flirtations, their little celebrations. They were good, decent, normal people.

I respect, and even admire, such people, but they are not the sort of people I can write stories about. I write stories about people who have some singularity of character which suggests to me that they may be capable of behaving in such a way as to give me an idea that I can make use of, or about people who by some accident or another, accident of temperament, accident of environment, have been involved in unusual contingencies. But, I repeat, they are the exception.

The Vessel of Wrath

THERE are few books in the world that contain more meat than the "Sailing Directions" published by the Hydrographic Department by order of the Lords Commissioners of the Admiralty. They are handsome volumes, bound (very flimsily) in cloth of different colours, and the most expensive of them is cheap. For four shillings you can buy the "Yangtse Kiang Pilot", 'containing a description of, and sailing directions for, the Yangtse Kiang from the Wusung river to the highest navigable point, including the Han Kiang, the Kialing Kiang, and the Min Kiang'; and for three shillings you can get Part III of the "Eastern Archipelago Pilot", 'comprising the N.E. end of Celebes, Molucca and Gilolo passages, Banda and Arafura Seas, and North, West, and South-West coasts of New Guinea.' But it is not very safe to do so if you are a creature of settled habits that you have no wish to disturb or if you have an occupation that holds you fast to one place. These business-like books take you upon enchanted journeys of the spirit; and their matter-of-fact style, the admirable order, the concision with which the material is set before you, the stern sense of the practical that informs every line, cannot dim the poetry that, like the spice-laden breeze that assails your senses with a more than material languor when you approach some of those magic islands of the Eastern seas, blows with so sweet a fragrance through the printed pages. They tell you the anchorages and the landing places, what supplies you can get at each spot, and where you can get water; they tell you the lights and buoys, tides, winds and weather that you will find there. They give you brief information about the population and the trade. And it is strange when you think how sedately it is all set down, with no words wasted, that so much else is given you besides. What? Well, mystery and beauty, romance and the glamour of the unknown. It is no common book that offers you casually turning its pages such a paragraph as this: 'Supplies. A few jungle fowl are preserved, the island is also the resort of vast numbers of sea birds. Turtle are found in the lagoon, as well as quantities of various fish, including grey mullet, shark, and dog-fish; the seine cannot be used with any effect; but there is a fish which may be taken on a rod. A small store of tinned provisions and spirits is kept in a hut for the relief of shipwrecked persons. Good water may be obtained from a well near the landing-place'. Can the imagination want more material than this to go on a journey through time and space?

In the volume from which I have copied this passage, the compilers with the same restraint have described the Alas Islands. They are composed of a group or chain of islands, 'for the most part low and wooded, extending about 75 miles east and west, and 40 miles north and south'. The information about them, you are told, is very slight; there are channels between the different groups, and several vessels have passed through them, but the passages have not been thoroughly explored, and the positions of many of the dangers not yet determined; it is therefore advisable to avoid them. The population of the group is estimated at about 8000, of whom 200 are Chinese and 400 Mohammedans. The rest are heathen. The principal island is called Baru, it is surrounded by a reef, and here lives a Dutch Contrôleur. His white house with its red roof on the top of a little hill is the most prominent object that the vessels of the Royal Netherlands Steam Packet Company see when every other month on their way up to Macassar and every four weeks on their way down to Merauke in Dutch New Guinea they touch at the island.

At a certain moment of the world's history the Contrôleur was Mynheer Evert Gruyter and he ruled the people who inhabited the Alas Islands with firmness tempered by a keen sense of the ridiculous. He had thought it a very good joke to be placed at the age of twenty-seven in a position of such consequence and at thirty he was still amused by it. There was no cable communication between his islands and Batavia, and the mail arrived after so long a delay that even if he asked advice, by the time he received it, it was useless, and so he equably did what he thought best and trusted to his good fortune to keep out of trouble with the authorities. He was very short, not more than five feet four in height, and extremely fat; he was of a florid complexion. For coolness' sake he kept his head shaved and his face was hairless. It was round and red. His eyebrows were so fair that you hardly saw them; and he had little twinkling blue eyes. He knew that he had no dignity, but for the sake of his position made up for it by dressing very dapperly. He never went to his office, nor sat in court, nor walked abroad but in spotless white. His stengahshifter, with its bright brass buttons, fitted him very tightly and displayed the shocking fact that, young though he was, he had a round and protruding belly. His good-humoured face shone with sweat and he constantly fanned himself with a palm-leaf fan.

But in his house Mr. Gruyter preferred to wear nothing but a sarong and then with his white podgy little body he looked like a fat funny boy of sixteen. He was an early riser and his breakfast was always ready for him at six. It never varied. It consisted of a slice of papaia, three cold fried eggs, Edam cheese, sliced thin, and a cup of black coffee. When he had eaten it, he smoked a large Dutch cigar, read the papers if he had not read them through and through already, and then dressed to go down to his office.

One morning while he was thus occupied his head boy came into his bedroom and told him that Tuan Jones wanted to know if he could see him. Mr. Gruyter was standing in front of a looking-glass. He had his trousers on and was admiring his smooth chest. He arched his back in order to throw it out and throw in his belly and with a good deal of satisfaction gave his breast three or four resounding slaps. It was a manly chest. When the boy brought the message he looked at his own eyes in the mirror and exchanged a slightly ironic smile with them. He asked himself what the devil his visitor could want. Evert Gruyter spoke English, Dutch and Malay with equal facility, but he thought in Dutch. He liked to do this. It seemed to him a pleasantly ribald language.

"Ask the tuan to wait and say I shall come directly." He put on his tunic, over his naked body, buttoned it up, and strutted into the sitting-room. The Rev. Owen Jones got up.

"Good-morning, Mr. Jones," said the Contrôleur. "Have you come in to have a peg with me before I start my day's work?"

Mr. Jones did not smile.

"I've come to see you upon a very distressing matter, Mr. Gruyter," he answered.

The Contrôleur was not disconcerted by his visitor's gravity nor depressed by his words. His little blue eyes beamed amiably.

"Sit down, my dear fellow, and have a cigar."

Mr. Gruyter knew quite well that the Rev. Owen Jones neither drank nor smoked, but it tickled something prankish in his nature to offer him a drink and a smoke whenever they met. Mr. Jones shook his head.

Mr. Jones was in charge of the Baptist Mission on the Alas Islands. His headquarters were at Baru, the largest of them, with the greatest population, but he had meeting-houses under the care of native helpers in several other islands of the group. He was a tall, thin melancholy man, with a long face, sallow and drawn, of about forty. His brown hair was already white on the temples and it receded from the forehead. This gave him a look of somewhat vacuous intellectuality. Mr. Gruyter both disliked and respected him. He disliked him because he was narrow-minded and dogmatic. Himself a cheerful pagan who liked the good things of the flesh and was determined to get as many of them as his circumstances permitted, he had no patience with a man who disapproved of them all. He thought the customs of the country suited its inhabitants and had no patience with the missionary's energetic efforts to destroy a way of life that for centuries had worked very well. He respected him because he was honest, zealous and good. Mr. Jones, an Australian of Welsh descent, was the only qualified doctor in the group and it was a comfort to know that if you fell ill you need not rely only on a Chinese practitioner, and none knew better than the Contrôleur how useful to all Mr. Jones's skill had been and with what charity he had given it. On the occasion of an epidemic of influenza the missionary had done the work of ten men and no storm short of a typhoon could prevent him from crossing to one island or another if his help was needed.

He lived with his sister in a little white house about half a mile from the village and when the Contrôleur had arrived, came on board to meet him and begged him to stay till he could get his own house in order. The Contrôleur had accepted and soon saw for himself with what simplicity the couple lived. It was more than he could stand. Tea at three sparse meals a day and when he lit his cigar Mr. Jones politely but firmly asked him to be good enough not to smoke, since both his sister and he strongly disapproved of it. In twenty-four hours Mr. Gruyter moved into his own house. He fled, with panic in his heart, as though from a plague-stricken city. The Contrôleur was fond of a joke and he liked to laugh; to be with a man who took your nonsense in deadly earnest and never even smiled at your best story was more than flesh and blood could stand. The Rev. Owen Jones was a worthy man, but as a companion he was impossible. His sister was worse. Neither had a sense of humour, but whereas the missionary was of a melancholy turn, doing his duty so conscientiously, with the obvious conviction that everything in the world was hopeless, Miss Jones was resolutely cheerful. She grimly looked on the bright side of things. With the ferocity of an avenging angel she sought out the good in her fellow-men. Miss Jones taught in the mission school and helped her brother in his medical work. When he did operations she gave the anæsthetic and was matron, dresser and nurse of the tiny hospital which on his own initiative Mr. Jones had added to the mission. But the Contrôleur was an obstinate little fellow and he never lost his capacity of extracting amusement from the Rev. Owen's dour struggle with the infirmities of human nature, and Miss Jones's ruthless optimism. He had to get his fun where he could. The Dutch boats came in three times in two months for a few hours and then he could have a good old crack with the captain and chief engineer, and once in a blue moon a pearling lugger came in from Thursday Island or Port Darwin and for two or three days he had a grand time. They were rough fellows, the pearlers, for the most part, but they were full of guts, and they had plenty of liquor on board, and good stories to tell, and the Contrôleur had them up to his house and gave them a fine dinner and the party was only counted a success if they were all too drunk to get back on the lugger again that night. But beside the missionary the only white man who lived on Baru was Ginger Ted, and he, of course, was a disgrace to civilisation. There was not a single thing to be said in his favour. He cast discredit on the white race. All the same, but for Ginger Ted the Controleur sometimes thought he would find life on the island of Baru almost more than he could bear.

Oddly enough it was on account of this scamp that Mr. Jones, when he should have been instructing the pagan young in the mysteries of the Baptist faith, was paying Mr. Gruyter this early visit.

"Sit down, Mr. Jones," said the Contrôleur. "What can I do for you?"

"Well, I've come to see you about the man they call Ginger Ted. What are you going to do now?"

"Why, what's happened?"

"Haven't you heard? I thought the sergeant would have told you."

"I don't encourage the members of my staff to come to my private house unless the matter is urgent," said the Contrôleur rather grandly. "I am unlike you, Mr. Jones, I only work in order to have leisure and I like to enjoy my leisure without disturbance."

But Mr. Jones did not care much for small talk and he was not interested in general reflections.

"There was a disgraceful row in one of the Chinese shops last night. Ginger Ted wrecked the place and half killed a Chinaman."

"Drunk again, I suppose," said the Contrôleur placidly.

"Naturally. When is he anything else? They sent for the police and he assaulted the sergeant. They had to have six men to get him to the jail."

"He's a hefty fellow," said the Contrôleur.

"I suppose you'll send him to Macassar."

Evert Gruyter returned the missionary's outraged look with a merry twinkle. He was no fool and he knew already what Mr. Jones was up to. It gave him considerable amusement to tease him a little.

"Fortunately my powers are wide enough to enable

me to deal with the situation myself," he answered.

"You have power to deport anyone you like, Mr. Gruyter, and I'm sure it would save a lot of trouble if you got rid of the man altogether."

"I have the power of course, but I am sure you would be the last person to wish me to use it arbitrarily."

"Mr. Gruyter, the man's presence here is a public scandal. He's never sober from morning till night; it's notorious that he has relations with one native woman after another."

"That is an interesting point, Mr. Jones. I had always heard that alcoholic excess, though it stimulated sexual desire, prevented its gratification. What you tell me about Ginger Ted does not seem to bear out this theory."

The missionary flushed a dull red.

"These are physiological matters which at the moment I have no wish to go into," he said, frigidly. "The behaviour of this man does incalculable damage to the prestige of the white race, and his example seriously hampers the efforts that are made in other quarters to induce the people of these islands to lead a less vicious life. He's an out-and-out bad lot."

"Pardon my asking, but have you made any attempts to reform him?"

"When he first drifted here I did my best to get in touch with him. He repelled all my advances. When there was that first trouble I went to him and talked to him straight from the shoulder. He swore at me."

"No one has a greater appreciation than I of the excellent work that you and other missionaries do on these islands, but are you sure that you always exercise your calling with all the tact possible?"

The Contrôleur was rather pleased with this phrase. It was extremely courteous and yet contained a reproof that he thought worth administering. The missionary looked at him gravely. His sad brown eyes were full of sincerity.

"Did Jesus exercise tact when he took a whip and drove the money-changers from the Temple? No, Mr. Gruyter. Tact is the subterfuge the lax avail themselves of to avoid doing their duty."

Mr. Jones's remark made the Contrôleur feel suddenly that he wanted a bottle of beer. The missionary leaned forward earnestly.

"Mr. Gruyter, you know this man's transgressions just as well as I do. It's unnecessary for me to remind you of them. There are no excuses for him. Now he really has overstepped the limit. You'll never have a better chance than this. I beg you to use the power you have and turn him out once for all."

The Contrôleur's eyes twinkled more brightly than ever. He was having a lot of fun. He reflected that human beings were much more amusing when you did not feel called upon in dealing with them to allot praise or blame.

"But, Mr. Jones, do I understand you right? Are you asking me to give you an assurance to deport this man before I've heard the evidence against him and listened to his defence?"

"I don't know what his defence can be."

The Contrôleur rose from his chair and really he managed to get quite a little dignity into his five feet four inches.

"I am here to administer justice according to the laws of the Dutch Government. Permit me to tell you that I am exceedingly surprised that you should attempt to influence me in my judicial functions."

The missionary was a trifle flustered. It had never occurred to him that this little whipper-snapper of a boy, ten years younger than himself, would dream of adopting such an attitude. He opened his mouth to explain and apologise, but the Contrôleur raised a podgy little hand.

"It is time for me to go to my office, Mr. Jones. I wish you good-morning."

The missionary, taken aback, bowed and without another word walked out of the room. He would have been surprised to see what the Contrôleur did when his back was turned. A broad grin broke on his lips and he put his thumb to his nose and cocked a snook at the Rev. Owen Jones.

A few minutes later he went down to his office. His head clerk, who was a Dutch half-caste, gave him his version of the previous night's row. It agreed pretty well with Mr. Jones's. The court was sitting that day.

"Will you take Ginger Ted first, sir?" asked the clerk.

"I see no reason to do that. There are two or three cases held over from the last sitting. I will take him in his proper order."

"I thought perhaps as he was a white man you would like to see him privately, sir."

"The majesty of the law knows no difference between white and coloured, my friend," said Mr. Gruyter, somewhat pompously.

The court was a big square room with wooden benches on which, crowded together, sat natives of all kinds, Polynesians, Bugis, Chinese, Malays and they all rose when a door was opened and a sergeant announced the arrival of the Contrôleur. He entered with his clerk and took his place on a little dais at a table of varnished pitch pine. Behind him was a large engraving of Queen Wilhelmina. He despatched half a dozen cases and then Ginger Ted was brought in. He stood in the dock, handcuffed, with a warder on either side of him. The Contrôleur looked at him with a grave face, but he could not keep the amusement out of his eyes.

Ginger Ted was suffering from a hang-over. He swayed a little as he stood and his eyes were vacant. He was a man still young, thirty perhaps, of somewhat over the middle height, rather fat, with a bloated red face and a shock of curly red hair. He had not come out of the tussle unscathed. He had a black eye and his mouth was cut and swollen. He wore khaki shorts, very dirty and ragged, and his singlet had been almost torn off his back. A great rent showed the thick mat of red hair with which his chest was covered, but showed also the astonishing whiteness of his skin. The Contrôleur looked at the charge sheet. He called the evidence. When he had heard it, when he had seen the Chinaman whose head Ginger Ted had broken with a bottle, when he had heard the agitated story of the sergeant who had been knocked flat when he tried to arrest him, when he had listened to the tale of the havoc wrought by Ginger Ted who in his drunken fury had smashed everything he could lay hands on, he turned and addressed the accused in English.

"Well, Ginger, what have you got to say for youself?"

"I was blind. I don't remember a thing about it. If they say I half killed 'im I suppose I did. I'll pay the damage if they'll give me time."

"You will, Ginger," said the Contrôleur, "but it's me who'll give you time."

He looked at Ginger Ted for a minute in silence. He was an unappetising object. A man who had gone completely to pieces. He was horrible. It made you shudder to look at him and if Mr. Jones had not been so officious, at that moment the Contrôleur would certainly have ordered him to be deported.

"You've been a trouble ever since you came to the islands, Ginger. You're a disgrace. You're incorrigibly idle. You've been picked up in the street dead drunk time and time again. You've kicked up row after row. You're hopeless. I told you the last time you were brought here that if you were arrested again I should deal with you severely. You've gone the limit this time and you're for it. I sentence you to six months' hard labour."

"Me?"

"You."

"By God, I'll kill you when I come out."

He burst into a string of oaths both filthy and blasphemous. Mr. Gruyter listened scornfully. You can swear much better in Dutch than in English and there was nothing that Ginger Ted said that he could not have effectively capped.

"Be quiet," he ordered. "You make me tired."

The Contrôleur repeated his sentence in Malay and the prisoner was led struggling away.

Mr. Gruyter sat down to tiffin in high good-humour. It was astonishing how amusing life could be if you exercised a little ingenuity. There were people in Amsterdam, and even in Batavia and Surabaya, who looked upon his island home as a place of exile. They little knew how agreeable it was and what fun he could extract from unpromising material. They asked him whether he did not miss the club and the races and the cinema, the dances that were held once a week at the Casino and the society of Dutch ladies. Not at all. He liked comfort. The substantial furniture of the room in which he sat had a satisfying solidity. He liked reading French novels of a frivolous nature and he appreciated the sensation of reading one after the other without the uneasiness occasioned by the thought that he was wasting his time. It seemed to him a great luxury to waste time. When his young man's fancy turned to thoughts of love his head boy brought to the house a little dark-skinned bright-eyed creature in a sarong. He took care to form no connection of a permanent nature. He thought that change kept the heart young. He enjoyed freedom and was not weighed down by a sense of responsibility. He did not mind the heat. It made a sluice over with cold water half a dozen times a day a pleasure that had almost an æsthetic quality. He played the piano. He wrote letters to his friends in Holland. He felt no need for the conversation of intellectual persons. He liked a good laugh, but he could get that out of a fool just as well as out of a professor of philosophy. He had a notion that he was a very wise little man.

Like all good Dutchmen in the Far East he began his lunch with a small glass of Hollands gin. It has a musty acrid flavour, and the taste for it must be acquired, but Mr. Gruyter preferred it to any cocktail. When he drank it he felt besides that he was upholding the traditions of his race. Then he had *rystafel*. He had it every day. He heaped a soup-plate high with rice, and then, his three boys waiting on him, helped himself to the curry that one handed him, to the fried egg that another brought, and to the condiment presented by the third. Then each one brought another dish, of bacon, or bananas, or pickled fish, and presently his plate was piled high in a huge pyramid. He stirred it all together and began to eat. He ate slowly and with relish. He drank a bottle of beer.

He did not think while he was eating. His attention was applied to the mass in front of him and he consumed it with a happy concentration. It never palled on him. And when he had emptied the great plate it was a compensation to think that next day he would have *rystafel* again. He grew tired of it as little as the rest of us grow tired of bread. He finished his beer and lit his cigar. The boy brought him a cup of coffee. He leaned back in his chair then and allowed himself the luxury of reflection.

It tickled him to have sentenced Ginger Ted to the richly deserved punishment of six months' hard labour, and he smiled when he thought of him working on the roads with the other prisoners. It would have been silly to deport from the island the one man with whom he could occasionally have a heart-to-heart talk, and besides, the satisfaction it would have given the missionary would have been bad for that gentleman's character. Ginger Ted was a scamp and a scallywag, but the Contrôleur had a kindly feeling for him. They had drunk many a bottle of beer in one another's company and when the pearl fishers from Port Darwin came in and they all made a night of it, they had got gloriously tight together. The Contrôleur liked the reckless way in which Ginger Ted squandered the priceless treasure of life.

Ginger Ted had wandered in one day on the ship that was going up from Merauke to Macassar. The captain did not know how he had found his way there, but he had travelled steerage with the natives, and he stopped off at the Alas Islands because he liked the look of them. Mr. Gruyter had a suspicion that their attraction consisted perhaps in their being under the Dutch flag and so out of British jurisdicion. But his papers were in order, so there was no reason why he should not stay. He said that he was buying pearl-shell for an Australian firm, but it soon appeared that his commercial undertakings were not serious. Drink, indeed, took up so much of his time that he had little left over for other pursuits. He was in receipt of two pounds a week, paid monthly, which came regularly to him from England. The Contrôleur guessed that this sum was paid only so long as he kept well away from the persons who sent it. It was anyway too small to permit him any liberty of movement. Ginger Ted was reticent. The Contrôleur discovered that he was an Englishman, this he learnt from his passport, which described him as Edward Wilson, and that he had been in Australia. But why he had left England and what he had done in Australia he had no notion. Nor could he ever quite tell to what class Ginger Ted belonged. When you saw him in a filthy singlet and a pair of ragged trousers,a battered topee on his head, with the pearl-fishers and heard his conversation, coarse, obscene and illiterate, you thought he must be a sailor before the mast who had deserted his ship, or a labourer, but when you saw his handwriting you were surprised to find that it was that of a man not without at least some education, and on occasion when you got him alone, if he had had a few drinks but was not yet drunk, he would talk of matters that neither a sailor nor a labourer would have been likely to know anything about. The Contrôleur had a certain sensitiveness and he realised that Ginger Ted did not speak to him as an inferior to a superior but as an equal. Most of his remittance was mortaged before he received it, and the Chinamen to whom he owed money were standing at his elbow when the monthly letter was delivered to him, but with what was left he proceeded to get drunk. It was then that he made trouble, for when drunk he grew violent and was then likely to commit acts that brought him into the hands of the police. Hitherto Mr. Gruyter had contented himself with keeping him in jail till he was sober and giving him a talking to. When he was out of money he cadged what drink he could from anyone who would give it him. Rum, brandy, arak, it was all the same to him. Two or three times Mr. Gruyter had got him work on plantations run by Chinese in one or other of the islands, but he could not stick to it, and in a few weeks was back again at Baru on the beach. It was a miracle how he kept body and soul together. He had, of course, a way with him. He picked up the various dialects spoken on the islands, and knew how to make the natives laugh. They despised him, but they respected his physical strength, and they liked his company. He was as a result never at a loss for a meal or a mat to sleep on. The strange thing was, and it was this that chiefly outraged the Rev. Owen Jones, that he could do anything he liked with a woman. The Contrôleur could not imagine what it was they saw in him. He was casual with them and rather brutal. He took what they gave him, but seemed incapable of gratitude. He used them for his pleasure and then flung them indifferently away. Once or twice this had got him into trouble, and Mr. Gruyter had had to sentence an angry father for sticking a knife in Ginger Ted's back one night, and a Chinese woman had sought to poison herself by swallowing opium because he had deserted her. Once Mr. Jones came to the Contrôleur in a great state because the beachcomber had seduced one of his converts. The Contrôleur agreed that it was very deplorable, but could only advise Mr. Jones to keep a sharp eye on these young persons. The Contrôleur liked it less when he discovered that a girl whom he fancied a good deal himself and had been seeing for several weeks had all the time been according her favours also to Ginger Ted. When he thought of this particular incident he smiled again at the thought of Ginger Ted doing six months' hard labour. It is seldom in this life that in the process of doing your bounden duty you can get back on a fellow who has played you a dirty trick.

A few days later Mr. Gruyter was taking a walk, partly for exercise and partly to see that some job he wanted done was being duly proceeded with, when he passed a gang of prisoners working under the charge of a warder. Among them he saw Ginger Ted. He wore the prison sarong, a dingy tunic called in Malay a *baju*, and his own battered topi. They were repairing the road, and Ginger Ted was wielding a heavy pick. The way was narrow and the Contrôleur saw that he must pass within a foot of him. He remembered his threats. He knew that Ginger Ted was a man of violent passion and the language he had used in the dock made it plain that he had not seen what a good joke it was of the Contrôleur's to sentence him to six months' hard labour. If Ginger Ted suddenly attacked him with the pick, nothing on God's earth could save him. It was true that the warder would immediately shoot him down, but meanwhile the Contrôleur's head would be bashed in. It was with a funny little feeling in the pit of his stomach that Mr. Gruyter walked through the gang of prisoners. They were working in pairs a few feet from one another. He set his mind on neither hastening his pace nor slackening it. As he passed Ginger Ted, the man swung his pick into the ground and looked up at the Contrôleur and as he caught his eye winked. The Contrôleur checked the smile that rose to his lips and with official dignity strode on. But that wink, so lusciously full of sardonic humour, filled him with satisfaction. If he had been the Caliph of Bagdad instead of a junior official in the Dutch Civil Service, he would forthwith have released Ginger Ted, sent slaves to bath and perfume him, and having clothed him in a golden robe entertained him to a sumptuous repast.

Ginger Ted was an exemplary prisoner and in a month or two the Contrôleur, having occasion to send a gang to do some work on one of the outlying islands, included him in it. There was no jail there, so the ten fellows he sent, under the charge of a warder, were billeted on the natives and after their day's work lived like free men. The job was sufficient to take up the rest of Ginger Ted's sentence. The Contrôleur saw him before he left.

"Look here, Ginger," he said to him, "here's ten guilder for you so that you can buy yourself tobacco when you're gone."

"Couldn't you make it a bit more? There's eight pounds a month coming in regularly."

"I think that's enough. I'll keep the letters that come for you, and when you get back you'll have a tidy sum. You'll have enough to take you anywhere you want to go."

"I'm very comfortable here," said Ginger Ted.

"Well, the day you come back, clean youself up and come over to my house. We'll have a bottle of beer together."

"That'll be fine. I guess I'll be ready for a good crack then."

Now chance steps in. The island to which Ginger Ted had been sent was called Maputiti, and like all the rest of them it was rocky, heavily wooded and surrounded by a reef. There was a village among coconuts on the sea-shore opposite the opening of the reef and another village on a brackish lake in the middle of the island. Of this some of the inhabitants had been converted to Christianity. Communication with Baru was effected by a launch that touched at the various islands at irregular intervals. It carried passengers and produce. But the villagers were seafaring folk, and if they had to communicate urgently with Baru, manned a prahu and sailed the fifty miles or so that separated them from it. It happened that when Ginger Ted's sentence had but another fortinight to run the Christian headman of the village on the lake was taken suddenly ill. The native remedies availed him nothing and he writhed in agony. Messengers were sent to Baru imploring the missionary's help; but as ill luck would have it Mr. Jones was suffering at the moment from an attack of malaria. He was in bed and unable to move. He talked the matter over with his sister.

"It sounds like acute appendicitis," he told her.

"You can't go, Owen," she said.

"I can't let the man die."

Mr. Jones had a temperature of a hundred and four. His head was aching like mad. He had been delirious all night. His eyes were shining strangely and his sister felt that he was holding on to his wits by a sheer effort of will.

"You couldn't operate in the state you're in."

"No, I couldn't. Then Hassan must go."

Hassan was the dispenser.

"You couldn't trust Hassan. He'd never dare to do an operation on his own responsibility. And they'd never let him. I'll go. Hassan can stay here and look after you."

"You can't remove an appendix?"

"Why not? I've seen you do it. I've done lots of minor operations."

Mr. Jones felt he didn't quite understand what she

was saying.

"Is the launch in?"

"No, it's gone to one of the islands. But I can go in the prahu the men came in."

"You? I wasn't thinking of you. You can't go."

"I'm going, Owen."

"Going where?" he said.

She saw that his mind was wandering already. She put her hand soothingly on his dry forehead. She gave him a dose of medicine. He muttered something and she realised that he did not know where he was. Of course she was anxious about him, but she knew that his illness was not dangerous, and she could leave him safely to the mission boy who was helping her nurse him and to the native dispenser. She slipped out of the room. She put her toilet things, a night-dress, and a change of clothes into a bag. A little chest with surgical instruments, bandages and antiseptic dressings was kept always ready. She gave them to the two natives who had come over from Maputiti, and telling the dispenser what she was going to do gave him instructions to inform her brother when he was able to listen. Above all he was not to be anxious about her. She put on her topee and sallied forth. The mission was about half a mile from the village. She walked quickly. At the end of the jetty the prahu was waiting. Six men manned it. She took her place in the stern and they set off with a rapid stroke. Within the reef the sea was calm, but when they crossed the bar they came upon a long swell. But this was not the first journey of the sort Miss Jones had taken and she was confident of the seaworthiness of the boat she was in. It was noon and the sun beat down from a sultry sky. The only thing that harassed her was that they could not arrive before dark, and if she found it necessary to operate at once she could count only on the light of hurricane lamps.

Miss Jones was a woman of hard on forty. Nothing in

her appearance would have prepared you for such determination as she had just shown. She had an odd drooping gracefulness, which suggested that she might be swayed by every breeze; it was almost an affectation; and it made the strength of character which you soon discovered in her seem positively monstrous. She was flat-chested, tall and extremely thin. She had a long sallow face and she was much afflicted with prickly heat. Her lank brown hair was drawn back straight from her forehead. She had rather small eyes, grey in colour, and because they were somewhat too close they gave her face a shrewish look. Her nose was long and thin and a trifle red. She suffered a good deal from indigestion. But this infirmity availed nothing against her ruthless determination to look upon the bright side of things. Firmly persuaded that the world was evil and men unspeakably vicious, she extracted any little piece of decency she could find in them with the modest pride with which a conjurer extracts a rabbit from a hat. She was quick, resourceful and competent. When she arrived on the island she saw that there was not a moment to lose if she was to save the headman's life. Under the greatest difficulties, showing a native how to give the anæsthetic, she operated, and for the next three days nursed the patient with anxious assiduity. Everything went very well and she realised that her brother could not have made a better job of it. She waited long enough to take out the stitches and then prepared to go home. She could flatter herself that she had not wasted her time. She had given medical attention to such as needed it, she had strengthened the small Christian community in its faith, admonished such as were lax and cast the good seed in places where it might be hoped under divine providence to take root.

The launch, coming from one of the other islands, put in somewhat late in the afternoon, but it was full moon and they expected to reach Baru before midnight.

They brought her things down to the wharf and the people who were seeing her off stood about repeating their thanks. Quite a little crowd collected. The launch was loaded with sacks of copra, but Miss Jones was used to its strong smell and it did not incommode her. She made herself as comfortable a place to sit in as she could, and waiting for the launch to start, chatted with her grateful flock. She was the only passenger. Suddenly a group of natives emerged from the trees that embowered the little village on the lagoon and she saw that among them was a white man. He wore a prison sarong and a baju. He had long red hair. She at once recognised Ginger Ted. A policeman was with him. They shook hands and Ginger Ted shook hands with the villagers who accompanied him. They bore bundles of fruit and a jar which Miss Jones guessed contained native spirit, and these they put in the launch. She discovered to her surprise that Ginger Ted was coming with her. His term was up and instructions had arrived that he was to be returned to Baru in the launch. He gave her a glance, but did not nod – indeed Miss Jones turned away her head – and stepped in. The mechanic started his engine and in a moment they were jug-jugging through the channel in the lagoon. Ginger Ted clambered on to a pile of sacks and lit a cigarette.

Miss Jones ignored him. Of course she knew him very well. Her heart sank when she thought that he was going to be once more in Baru, creating a scandal and drinking, a peril to the women and a thorn in the flesh of all decent people. She knew the steps her brother had taken to have him deported and she had no patience with the Contrôleur, who would not see a duty that stared him so plainly in the face. When they had crossed the bar and were in the open sea Ginger Ted took the stopper out of the jar of arak and putting his mouth to it took a long pull. Then he handed the jar to the two mechanics who formed the crew. One was a middle-aged man and the other a youth.

"I do not wish you to drink anything while we are on the journey," said Miss Jones sternly to the elder one.

He smiled at her and drank.

"A little arak can do no one any harm," he answered. He passed the jar to his companion, who drank also.

"If you drink again I shall complain to the Contrôleur," said Miss Jones.

The elder man said something she could not understand, but which she suspected was very rude, and passed the jar back to Ginger Ted. They went along for an hour or more. The sea was like glass and the sun set radiantly. It set behind one of the islands and for a few minutes changed it into a mystic city of the skies. Miss Jones turned round to watch it and her heart was filled with gratitude for the beauty of the world.

"And only man is vile," she quoted to herself.

They went due east. In the distance was a little island which she knew they passed close by. It was uninhabited. A rocky islet thickly grown with virgin forest. The boatman lit his lamps. The night fell and immediately the sky was thick with stars. The moon had not yet risen. Suddenly there was a slight jar and the launch began to vibrate strangely. The engine rattled. The head mechanic, calling to his mate to take the helm, crept under the housing. They seemed to be going more slowly. The engine stopped. She asked the youth what was the matter, but he did not know. Ginger Ted got down from the top of the copra sacks and slipped under the housing. When he reappeared she would have liked to ask him what had happened, but her dignity prevented her. She sat still and occupied herself with her thoughts. There was a long swell and the launch rolled slightly. The mechanic emerged once more into view and started the engine. Though it rattled like mad they began to move. The launch vibrated from stem to stern. They went very slowly. Evidently something was amiss, but

Miss Jones was exasperated rather than alarmed. The launch was supposed to do six knots, but now it was just crawling along; at that rate they would not get into Baru till long, long after midnight. The mechanic, still busy under the housing, shouted out something to the man at the helm. They spoke in Bugi, of which Miss Jones knew very little. But after a while she noticed that they had changed their course and seemed to be heading for the little uninhabited island a good deal to the lee of which they should have passed.

"Where are we going?" she asked the helmsman with sudden misgiving.

He pointed to the islet. She got up and went to the housing and called to the man to come out.

"You're not going there? Why? What's the matter?"

"I can't get to Baru," he said.

"But you must. I insist. I order you to go to Baru."

The man shrugged his shoulders. He turned his back on her and slipped once more under the housing. Then Ginger Ted addressed her.

"One of the blades of the propeller has broken off. He thinks he can get as far as that island. We shall have to stay the night there and he'll put on a new propeller in the morning when the tide's out."

"I can't spend the night on an uninhabited island with three men," she cried.

"A lot of women would jump at it."

"I insist on going to Baru. Whatever happens we must get there to-night."

"Don't get excited, old girl. We've got to beach the boat to put a new propeller on, and we shall be all right on the island."

"How dare you speak to me like that! I think you're very insolent."

"You'll be O.K. We've got plenty of grub and we'll have a snack when we land. You have a drop of arak and you'll feel like a house on fire."

"You're an impertinent man. If you don't go to Baru I'll have you all put in prison."

"We're not going to Baru. We can't. We're going to that island and if you don't like it you can get out and swim."

"Oh, you'll pay for this."

"Shut up, you old cow," said Ginger Ted.

Miss Jones gave a gasp of anger. But she controlled herself. Even out there, in the middle of the ocean, she had too much dignity to bandy words with that vile wretch. The launch, the engine rattling horribly, crawled on. It was pitch dark now, and she could no longer see the island they were making for. Miss Jones, deeply incensed, sat with lips tight shut and a frown on her brow; she was not used to being crossed. Then the moon rose and she could see the bulk of Ginger Ted sprawling on the top of the piled sacks of copra. The glimmer of his cigarette was strangely sinister. Now the island was vaguely outlined against the sky. They reached it and the boatman ran the launch on to the beach. Suddenly Miss Jones gave a gasp. The truth had dawned on her and her anger changed to fear. Her heart beat violently. She shook in every limb. She felt dreadfully faint. She saw it all. Was the broken propeller a put-up job or was it an accident? She could not be certain; anyhow, she knew that Ginger Ted would seize the opportunity. Ginger Ted would rape her. She knew his character. He was mad about women. That was what he had done, practically, to the girl at the mission, such a good little thing she was and an excellent sempstress; they would have prosecuted him for that and he would have been sentenced to years of imprisonment only very unfortunately the innocent child had gone back to him several times and indeed had only complained of his ill usage when he left her for somebody else. They had gone to the Contrôleur about it, but he had refused to take any steps, saying in that coarse way of his that even if what the girl said was true, it didn't look very much as though it had been an altogether unpleasant experience. Ginger Ted was a scoundrel. And she was a white woman. What chance was there that he would spare her? None. She knew men. But she must pull herself together. She must keep her wits about her. She must have courage. She was determined to sell her virtue dearly, and if he killed her – well, she would rather die than yield. And if she died she would rest in the arms of Jesus. For a moment a great light blinded her eyes and she saw the mansions of her Heavenly Father. They were a grand and sumptuous mixture of a picture palace and a railway station. The mechanics and Ginger Ted jumped out of the launch and, waist-deep in water, gathered round the broken propeller. She took advantage of their preoccupation to get her case of surgical instruments out of the box. She took out the four scalpels it contained and secreted them in her clothing. If Ginger Ted touched her she would not hesitate to plunge a scalpel in his heart.

"Now then, miss, you'd better get out," said Ginger Ted. "You'll be better off on the beach than in the boat."

She thought so too. At least there she would have freedom of action. Without a word she clambered over the copra sacks. He offered her his hand.

"I don't want your help," she said coldly.

"You can go to hell," he answered.

It was a little difficult to get out of the boat without showing her legs, but by the exercise of considerable ingenuity she managed it.

"Damned lucky we've got something to eat. We'll make a fire and then you'd better have a snack and a nip of arak."

"I want nothing. I only want to be left alone."

"It won't hurt me if you go hungry."

She did not answer. She walked, with head erect, along the beach. She held the largest scalpel in her closed fist. The moon allowed her to see where she was going. She looked for a place to hide. The thick forest came down to the very edge of the beach; but, afraid of its darkness (after all, she was but a woman), she dared not plunge into its depth. She did not know what animals lurked there or what dangerous snakes. Besides, her instinct told her that it was better to keep those three bad men in sight; then if they came towards her she would be prepared. Presently she found a little hollow. She looked round. They seemed to be occupied with their own affairs and they could not see her. She slipped in. There was a rock between them and her so that she was hidden from them and yet could watch them. She saw them go to and from the boat carrying things. She saw them build a fire. It lit them luridly and she saw them sit around it and eat, and she saw the jar of arak passed from one to the other. They were all going to get drunk. What would happen to her then? It might be that she could cope with Ginger Ted, though his strength terrified her, but against three she would be powerless. A mad idea came to her to go to Ginger Ted and fall on her knees before him and beg him to spare her. He must have some spark of decent feeling in him and she had always been so convinced that there was good even in the worst of men. He must have had a mother. Perhaps he had a sister. Ah, but how could you appeal to a man blinded with lust and drunk with arak? She began to feel terribly weak. She was afraid she was going to cry. That would never do. She needed all her self-control. She bit her lip. She watched them, like a tiger watching his prey; no, not like that, like a lamb watching three hungry wolves. She saw them put more wood on the fire, and Ginger Ted, in his sarong, silhouetted by the flames. Perhaps after he had had his will of her he would pass her on to the others. How could she go back to her brother when such a thing had happened to her? Of course he would be sympathetic, but would he ever feel quite the same to her again? It would break his heart. And perhaps he would think that she ought to have resisted more. For his sake perhaps it would be better if she said nothing about it. Naturally the men would say nothing. It would mean twenty years in prison for them. But then supposing she had a baby. Miss Jones instinctively clenched her hands with horror and nearly cut herself with the scalpel. Of course it would only infuriate them if she resisted.

"What shall I do?" she cried. "What have I done to deserve this?"

She flung herself down on her knees and prayed to God to save her. She prayed long and earnestly. She reminded God that she was a virgin and just mentioned, in case it had slipped the divine memory, how much St. Paul had valued that excellent state. And then she peeped round the rock again. The three men appeared to be smoking and the fire was dying down. Now was the time that Ginger Ted's lewd thoughts might be expected to turn to the woman who was at his mercy. She smothered a cry, for suddenly he got up and walked in her direction. She felt all her muscles grow taut, and though her heart was beating furiously she clenched the scalpel firmly in her hand. But it was for another purpose that Ginger Ted had got up. Miss Jones blushed and looked away. He strolled slowly back to the others and sitting down again raised the jar of arak to his lips. Miss Jones, crouching behind the rock, watched with straining eyes. The conversation round the fire grew less and presently she divined, rather than saw, that the two natives wrapped themselves in blankets and composed themselves to slumber. She understood. This was the moment Ginger Ted had been waiting for. When they were fast asleep he would get up cautiously and without a sound, in order not to wake the others, creep stealthily towards her. Was it that he was unwilling to share her with them or did he know that his deed was so dastardly that he did not wish them to know of it? After all, he was a white man and she was a white woman. He could not have sunk so low as to allow her to suffer the violence of natives. But his plan, which was so obvious to her, had given her an idea; when she saw him coming she would scream, she would scream so loudly that it would wake the two mechanics. She remembered now that the elder, though he had only one eye, had a kind face. But Ginger Ted did not move. She was feeling terribly tired. She began to fear that she would not have the strength now to resist him. She had gone through too much. She closed her eyes for a minute.

When she opened them it was broad daylight. She must have fallen asleep and, so shattered was she by emotion, have slept till long after dawn. It gave her quite a turn. She sought to rise, but something caught in her legs. She looked and found that she was covered with two empty copra sacks. Someone had come in the night and put them over her. Ginger Ted! She gave a little scream. The horrible thought flashed through her mind that he had outraged her in her sleep. No. It was impossible. And yet he had had her at his mercy. Defenceless. And he had spared her. She blushed furiously. She raised herself to her feet, feeling a little stiff, and arranged her disordered dress. The scalpel had fallen from her hand and she picked it up. She took the two copra sacks and emerged from her hiding-place. She walked towards the boat. It was floating in the shallow water of the lagoon.

"Come on, Miss Jones," said Ginger Ted. "We've finished. I was just going to wake you up."

She could not look at him, but she felt herself as red as a turkey cock.

"Have a banana?" he said.

Without a word she took it. She was very hungry, and ate it with relish.

"Step on this rock and you'll be able to get in without

wetting your feet."

Miss Jones felt as though she could sink into the ground with shame, but she did as he told her. He took hold of her arm – good heavens! his hand was like an iron vice, never, never could she have struggled with him – and helped her into the launch. The mechanic started the engine and they slid out of the lagoon. In three hours they were at Baru.

That evening, having been officially released, Ginger Ted went to the Contrôleur's house. He wore no longer the prison uniform, but the ragged singlet and the khaki shorts in which he had been arrested. He had had his hair cut and it fitted his head now like a little curly red cap. He was thinner. He had lost his bloated flabbiness and looked younger and better. Mr. Gruyter, a friendly grin on his round face, shook hands with him and asked him to sit down. The boy brought two bottles of beer.

"I'm glad to see you hadn't forgotten my invitation, Ginger," said the Contrôleur.

"Not likely. I've been looking forward to this for six months."

"Here's luck, Ginger Ted."

"Same to you, Contrôleur."

They emptied their glasses and the Contrôleur clapped his hands. The boy brought two more bottles.

"Well, you don't bear me any malice for the sentence I gave you, I hope."

"No bloody fear. I was mad for a minute, but I got over it. I didn't have half a bad time, you know. Nice lot of girls on that island, Contrôleur. You ought to give 'em a look over one of these days."

"You're a bad lot, Ginger."

"Terrible."

"Good beer, isn't it?"

"Fine."

"Let's have some more."

Ginger Ted's remittance had been arriving every month and the Contrôleur now had fifty pounds for him. When the damage he had done to the Chinaman's shop was paid for there would still be over thirty.

"That's quite a lot of money, Ginger. You ought to do something useful with it."

"I mean to," answered Ginger. "Spend it."

The Contrôleur sighed.

"Well, that's what money's for, I guess."

The Contrôleur gave his guest the news. Not much had happened during the last six months. Time on the Alas Islands did not matter very much and the rest of the world did not matter at all.

"Any wars anywhere?" asked Ginger Ted.

"No. Not that I've noticed. Harry Jervis found a pretty big pearl. He says he's going to ask a thousand quid for it."

"I hope he gets it."

"And Charlie McCormack's married."

"He always was a bit soft."

Suddenly the boy appeared and said Mr. Jones wished to know if he might come in. Before the Contrôleur could give an answer Mr. Jones walked in.

"I won't detain you long," he said. "I've been trying to get hold of this good man all day and when I heard he was here I thought you wouldn't mind my coming."

"How is Miss Jones?" asked the Contrôleur politely. "None the worse for her night in the open, I trust."

"She's naturally a bit shaken. She had a temperature and I've insisted on her going to bed, but I don't think it's serious."

The two men had got up on the missionary's entrance, and now the missionary went up to Ginger Ted and held out his hand.

"I want to thank you. You did a great and noble thing. My sister is right, one should always look for the good in their fellow-men; I am afraid I misjudged you in the past: I beg your pardon."

He spoke very solemnly. Ginger Ted looked at him with amazement. He had not been able to prevent the missionary taking his hand. He still held it.

"What the hell are you talking about?"

"You had my sister at your mercy and you spared her. I thought you were all evil and I am ashamed. She was defenceless. She was in your power. You had pity on her. I thank you from the bottom of my heart. Neither my sister nor I will ever forget. God bless and guard you always."

Mr. Jones's voice shook a little and he turned his head away. He released Ginger Ted's hand and strode quickly to the door. Ginger Ted watched him with a blank face.

"What the blazes does he mean?" he asked.

The Contrôleur laughed. He tried to control himself, but the more he did the more he laughed. He shook and you saw the folds of his fat belly ripple under the sarong. He leaned back in his long chair and rolled from side to side. He did not laugh only with his face, he laughed with his whole body, and even the muscles of his podgy legs shook with mirth. He held his aching ribs. Ginger Ted looked at him frowning, and because he did not understand what the joke was he grew angry. He seized one of the empty beer bottles by the neck.

"If you don't stop laughing, I'll break your bloody head open," he said.

The Contrôleur mopped his face. He swallowed a mouthful of beer. He sighed and groaned because his sides were hurting him.

"He's thanking you for having respected the virtue of Miss Jones," he spluttered at last.

"Me?" cried Ginger Ted.

The thought took quite a long time to travel through his head, but when at last he got it he flew into a violent rage. There flowed from his mouth such a stream of blasphemous obscenities as would have startled a marine.

"That old cow," he finished. "What does he take me for?"

"You have the reputation of being rather hot stuff with the girls, Ginger," giggled the little Contrôleur.

"I wouldn't touch her with the fag-end of a barge-pole. It never entered my head. The nerve. I'll wring his blasted neck. Look here, give me my money, I'm going to get drunk."

"I don't blame you," said the Contrôleur.

"That old cow," repeated Ginger Ted. "That old cow."

He was shocked and outraged. The suggestion really shattered his sense of decency.

The Contrôleur had the money at hand and having got Ginger Ted to sign the necessary papers gave it to him.

"Go and get drunk, Ginger Ted," he said, "but I warn you, if you get into mischief it'll be twelve months' next time."

"I shan't get into mischief," said Ginger Ted sombrely. He was suffering from a sense of injury. "It's an insult," he shouted at the Contrôleur. "That's what it is, it's a bloody insult."

He lurched out of the house, and as he went he muttered to himself: "Dirty swine, dirty swine." Ginger Ted remained drunk for a week. Mr. Jones went to see the Contrôleur again.

"I'm very sorry to hear that poor fellow has taken up his evil course again," he said. "My sister and I are dreadfully disappointed. I'm afraid it wasn't very wise to give him so much money at once."

"It was his own money. I had no right to keep it back."

"Not a legal right, perhaps, but surely a moral right."

He told the Contrôleur the story of that fearful night on the island. With her feminine instinct, Miss Jones had realised that the man, inflamed with lust, was determined to take advantage of her, and, resolved to defend herself to the last, had armed herself with a scalpel. He told the Contrôleur how she had prayed and wept and how she had hidden herself. Her agony was indescribable, and she knew that she could never have survived the shame. She rocked to and fro and every moment she thought he was coming. And there was no help anywhere and at last she had fallen asleep; she was tired out, poor thing, she had undergone more than any human being could stand, and then when she awoke she found that he had covered her with copra sacks. He had found her asleep, and surely it was her innocence, her very helplessness that had moved him, he hadn't the heart to touch her; he covered her gently with two copra sacks and crept silently away.

"It shows you that deep down in him there is something sterling. My sister feels it's our duty to save him. We must do something for him."

"Well, in your place I wouldn't try till he's got through all his money," said the Contrôleur, "and then if he's not in jail you can do what you like."

But Ginger Ted didn't want to be saved. About a fortnight after his release from prison he was sitting on a stool outside a Chinaman's shop looking vacantly down the street when he saw Miss Jones coming along. He stared at her for a minute and once more amazement seized him. He muttered to himself and there can be little doubt that his mutterings were disrespectful. But then he noticed that Miss Jones had seen him and he quickly turned his head away; he was conscious, notwithstanding, that she was looking at him. She was walking briskly, but she sensibly diminished her pace as she approached him. He thought she was going to stop and speak to him. He got up quickly and went into the shop. He did not venture to come out for at least five minutes. Half an hour later Mr. Jones himself came along and he went straight up to Ginger Ted with outstretched hand.

"How do you do, Mr. Edward? My sister told me I should find you here."

Ginger Ted gave him a surly look and did not take the proffered hand. He made no answer.

"We'd be so very glad if you'd come to dinner with us next Sunday. My sister's a capital cook and she'll make you a real Australian dinner."

"Go to hell," said Ginger Ted.

"That's not very gracious," said the missionary, but with a little laugh to show that he was not affronted. "You go and see the Contrôleur from time to time, why shouldn't you come and see us? It's pleasant to talk to white people now and then. Won't you let bygones be bygones? I can assure you of a very cordial welcome."

"I haven't got clothes fit to go out in," said Ginger Ted sulkily.

"Oh, never mind about that. Come as you are."

"I won't."

"Why not? You must have a reason."

Ginger Ted was a blunt man. He had no hesitation in saying what we should all like to when we receive unwelcome invitations.

"I don't want to."

"I'm sorry. My sister will be very disappointed."

Mr. Jones, determined to show that he was not in the least offended, gave him a breezy nod and walked on. Forty-eight hours later there mysteriouly arrived at the house in which Ginger Ted lodged a parcel containing a suit of ducks, a tennis shirt, a pair of socks and some shoes. He was unaccustomed to receiving presents and next time he saw the Contrôleur asked him if it was he who had sent the things.

"Not on your life," replied the Contrôleur. "I'm perfectly indifferent to the state of your wardrobe."

"Well, then, who the hell can have?"

"Search me."

It was necessary from time to time for Miss Jones to see Mr. Gruyter on business and shortly after this she came to see him one morning in his office. She was a capable woman and though she generally wanted him to do something he had no mind to, she did not waste his time. He was a little surprised then to discover that she had come on a very trivial errand. When he told her that he could not take cognizance of the matter in question, she did not as was her habit try to convince him, but accepted his refusal as definite. She got up to go and then as though it were an afterthought said:

"Oh, Mr. Gruyter, my brother is very anxious that we should have the man they call Ginger Ted to supper with us and I've written him a little note inviting him for the day after to-morrow. I think he's rather shy, and I wonder if you'd come with him."

"That's very kind of you."

"My brother feels that we ought to do something for the poor fellow."

"A woman's influence and all that sort of thing," said the Contrôleur demurely.

"Will you persuade him to come? I'm sure he will if you make a point of it, and when he knows the way he'll come again. It seems such a pity to let a young man like that go to pieces altogether."

The Contrôleur looked up at her. She was several inches taller than he. He thought her very unattractive. She reminded him strangely of wet linen hung on a clothes-line to dry. His eyes twinkled, but he kept a straight face.

"I'll do my best," he said.

"How old is he?" she asked.

"According to his passport he's thirty-one."

"And what is his real name?"

"Wilson."

"Edward Wilson," she said softly.

"It's astonishing that after the life he's led he should be so strong," murmured the Contrôleur. "He has the strength of an ox."

"Those red-headed men sometimes are very powerful," said Miss Jones, but spoke as though she were choking.

"Quite so," said the Contrôleur.

Then for no obvious reason Miss Jones blushed. She hurriedly said good-bye to the Contrôleur and left his office.

"*Godverdomme!*" said the Contrôleur.

He knew now who had sent Ginger Ted the new clothes.

He met him during the course of the day and asked him whether he had heard from Miss Jones. Ginger Ted took a crumpled ball of paper out of his pocket and gave it to him. It was the invitation. It ran as follows:

Dear Mr. Wilson,

My brother and I would be so very glad if you would come and have supper with us next Thursday at 7.30. The Contrôleur has kindly promised to come. We have some new records from Australia which I am sure you will like. I am afraid I was not very nice to you last time we met, but I did not know you so well then, and I am big enough to admit it when I have committed an error. I hope you will forgive me and let me be your friend.

Yours sincerely,
Martha Jones

The Contrôleur noticed that she addressed him as Mr. Wilson and referred to his own promise to go, so that when she told him she had already invited Ginger Ted she had a little anticipated the truth.

"What are you going to do?"

"I'm not going, if that's what you mean. Damned nerve."

"You must answer the letter."

"Well, I won't."

"Now look here, Ginger, you put on those new clothes and you come as a favour to me. I've got to go and, damn it all, you can't leave me in the lurch. It won't hurt you just once."

Ginger Ted looked at the Contrôleur suspiciously, but his face was serious and his manner sincere: he could not guess that within him the Dutchman bubbled with laughter.

"What the devil do they want me for?"

"I don't know. The pleasure of your society, I suppose."

"Will there be any booze?"

"No, but come up to my house at seven, and we'll have a tiddly before we go."

"Oh, all right," said Ginger Ted sulkily.

The Contrôleur rubbed his little fat hands with joy. He was expecting a great deal of amusement from the party. But when Thursday came and seven o'clock, Ginger Ted was dead drunk and Mr. Gruyter had to go alone. He told the missionary and his sister the plain truth. Mr. Jones shook his head.

"I'm afraid it's no good, Martha, the man's hopeless."

For a moment Miss Jones was silent and the Contrôleur saw two tears trickle down her long thin nose. She bit her lip.

"No one is hopeless. Everyone has some good in him. I shall pray for him every night. It would be wicked to doubt the power of God."

Perhaps Miss Jones was right in this, but the divine providence took a very funny way of effecting its ends. Ginger Ted began to drink more heavily than ever. He was so troublesome that even Mr. Gruyter lost patience with him. He made up his mind that he could not have the fellow on the islands any more and resolved to deport him on the next boat that touched at Baru. Then a man died under mysterious circumstances after having been for a trip to one of the islands and the Contrôleur learnt that there had been several deaths on the same island. He sent the Chinese who was the official doctor of the group to look into the matter, and very soon received intelligence that the deaths were due to cholera. Two more took place at Baru and the certainty was forced upon him that there was an epidemic.

The Contrôleur cursed freely. He cursed in Dutch, he cursed in English and he cursed in Malay. Then he drank a bottle of beer and smoked a cigar. After that he took thought. He knew the Chinese doctor would be useless. He was a nervous little man from Java and the natives would refuse to obey his orders. The Contrôleur was efficient and knew pretty well what must be done, but he could not do everything single-handed. He did not like Mr. Jones, but just then he was thankful that he was at hand, and he sent for him at once. He was accompanied by his sister.

"You know what I want to see you about, Mr. Jones," He said abruptly.

"Yes. I've been expecting a message from you. That is why my sister has come with me. We are ready to put all our resources at your disposal. I need not tell you that my sister is as competent as a man."

"I know. I shall be very glad of her assistance."

They set to without further delay to discuss the steps that must be taken. Hospital huts would have to be erected and quarantine stations. The inhabitants of the various villages on the islands must be forced to take proper precautions. In a good many cases the infected villages drew their water from the same well as the uninfected, and in each case this difficulty would have to be dealt with according to circumstances. It was necessary to send round people to give orders and make sure that they were carried out. Negligence must be ruthlessly punished. The worst of it was that the natives would not obey other natives, and orders given by native policemen, themselves unconvinced of their efficacy, would certainly be disregarded. It was advisable for Mr. Jones to stay at Baru, where the population was largest and his medical attention most wanted; and what with the official duties that forced him to keep in touch with his headquarters, it was impossible for Mr. Gruyter to visit all the other islands himself. Miss Jones must go; but the natives of some of the outlying islands were wild and treacherous; the Contrôleur had had a good deal of trouble with them. He did not like the idea of exposing her to danger.

"I'm not afraid," she said.

"I daresay. But if you have your throat cut I shall get into trouble, and besides, we're so short-handed I don't want to risk losing your help."

"Then let Mr. Wilson come with me. He knows the natives better than anyone and can speak all their dialects."

"Ginger Ted?" The Contrôleur stared at her. "He's just getting over an attack of D.Ts."

"I know," she answered.

"You know a great deal, Miss Jones."

Even though the moment was so serious Mr. Gruyter could not but smile. He gave her a sharp look, but she met it coolly.

"There's nothing like responsibility for bringing out what there is in a man, and I think something like this may be the making of him."

"Do you think it would be wise to trust yourself for days at a time to a man of such infamous character?" said the missionary.

"I put my trust in God," she answered gravely.

"Do you think he'd be any use?" asked the Contrôleur. "You know what he is."

"I'm convinced of it." Then she blushed. "After all, no one knows better than I that he's capable of self-control."

The Contrôleur bit his lip.

"Let's send for him."

He gave a message to the sergeant and in a few minutes Ginger Ted stood before them. He looked ill. He had evidently been much shaken by his recent attack and his nerves were all to pieces. He was in rags and he had not shaved for a week. No one could have looked more disreputable.

"Look here, Ginger," said the Contrôleur, "it's about this cholera business. We've got to force the natives to take precautions and we want you to help us."

"Why the hell should I?"

"No reason at all. Except philanthropy."

"Nothing doing, Contrôleur. I'm not a philanthropist."

"That settles that. That was all. You can go."

But as Ginger Ted turned to the door Miss Jones stopped him.

"It was my suggestion, Mr. Wilson. You see, they want me to go to Labobo and Sakunchi, and the natives there are so funny I was afraid to go alone. I thought if you came I should be safer."

He gave her a look of extreme distaste.

"What do you suppose I care if they cut your throat?"

Miss Jones looked at him and her eyes filled with tears. She began to cry. He stood and watched her stupidly.

"There's no reason why you should." She pulled herself together and dried her eyes. "I'm being silly. I shall be all right. I'll go alone."

"It's damned foolishness for a woman to go to Labobo."

She gave him a little smile.

"I daresay it is, but, you see, it's my job and I can't help myself. I'm sorry if I offended you by asking you. You must forget about it. I daresay it wasn't quite fair to ask you to take such a risk."

For quite a minute Ginger Ted stood and looked at her. He shifted from one foot to the other. His surly face seemed to grow black.

"Oh, hell, have it your own way," he said at last. "I'll come with you. When d'you want to start?"

They set out next day, with drugs and disinfectants, in the Government launch. Mr. Gruyter as soon as he had put the necessary work in order was to start off in a prahu in the other direction. For four months the epidemic raged. Though everything possible was done to localise it one island after another was attacked. The Contrôleur was busy from morning to night. He had no sooner got back to Baru from one or other of the islands to do what was necessary there than he had to set off again. He distributed food and medicine. He cheered the terrified people. He supervised everything. He worked like a dog. He saw nothing of Ginger Ted, but he heard from Mr. Jones that the experiment was working out beyond all hopes. The scamp was behaving himself. He had a way with the natives; and by cajolery, firmness and on occasion the use of his fist, managed to make them take the steps necessary for their own safety. Miss Jones could congratulate herself on the success of the scheme. But the Contrôleur was too tired to be amused. When the epidemic had run its course he rejoiced because out of a population of eight thousand only six hundred had died.

Finally he was able to give the district a clean bill of health.

One evening he was sitting in his sarong on the verandah of his house and he read a French novel with the happy consciousness that once more he could take things easy. His head boy came in and told him that Ginger Ted wished to see him. He got up from his chair and shouted to him to come in. Company was just what he wanted. It had crossed the Contrôleur's mind that it would be pleasant to get drunk that night, but it is dull to get drunk alone, and he had regretfully put the thought aside. And heaven had sent Ginger Ted in the nick of time. By God, they would make a night of it. After four months they deserved a bit of fun. Ginger Ted entered. He was wearing a clean suit of white ducks. He was shaved. He looked another man.

"Why, Ginger, you look as if you'd been spending a month at a health resort instead of nursing a pack of natives dying of cholera. And look at your clothes. Have you just stepped out of a band-box?"

Ginger Ted smiled rather sheepishly. The head boy brought two bottles of beer and poured them out.

"Help yourself, Ginger," said the Contrôleur as he took his glass.

"I don't think I'll have any, thank you."

The Contrôleur put down his glass and looked at Ginger Ted with amazement.

"Why, what's the matter? Aren't you thirsty?"

"I don't mind having a cup of tea."

"A cup of what?"

"I'm on the wagon. Martha and I are going to be married."

"Ginger!"

The Contrôleur's eyes popped out of his head. He scratched his shaven pate.

"You can't marry Miss Jones," he said. "No one could marry Miss Jones."

"Well, I'm going to. That's what I've come to see you about. Owen's going to marry us in chapel, but we want to be married by Dutch law as well."

"A joke's a joke, Ginger. What's the idea?"

"She wanted it. She fell for me that night we spent on the island when the propeller broke. She's not a bad old girl when you get to know her. It's her last chance, if you understand what I mean, and I'd like to do something to oblige her. And she wants someone to take care of her, there's no doubt about that."

"Ginger, Ginger, before you can say knife she'll make you into a damned missionary."

"I don't know that I'd mind that so much if we had a little mission of our own. She says I'm a bloody marvel with the natives. She says I can do more with a native in five minutes than Owen can do in a year. She says she's never known anyone with the magnetism I have. It seems a pity to waste a gift like that."

The Contrôleur looked at him without speaking and slowly nodded his head three or four times. She'd nobbled him all right.

"I've converted seventeen already," said Ginger Ted.

"You? I didn't know you believed in Christianity."

"Well, I don't know that I did exactly, but when I talked to 'em and they just came into the fold like a lot of blasted sheep, well, it gave me quite a turn. Blimey, I said, I daresay there's something in it after all."

"You should have raped her, Ginger, I wouldn't have been hard on you. I wouldn't have given you more than three years' and three years' is soon over."

"Look here, Contrôleur, don't you ever let on that the thought never entered my head. Women are touchy, you know, and she'd be as sore as hell if she knew that."

"I guessed she'd got her eye on you, but I never thought it would come to this." The Contrôleur in an agitated manner walked up and down the verandah. "Listen to me, old boy," he said after an interval of reflection, "we've had some grand times together and a friend's a friend. I'll tell you what I'll do, I'll lend you the launch and you can go and hide on one of the islands till the next ship comes along and then I'll get 'em to slow down and take you on board. You've only got one chance now and that's to cut and run."

Ginger Ted shook his head.

"It's no good, Contrôleur, I know you mean well, but I'm going to marry the blasted woman, and that's that. You don't know the joy of bringing all them bleeding sinners to repentance, and Christ! that girl can make a treacle pudding. I haven't eaten a better one since I was a kid."

The Contrôleur was very much disturbed. The drunken scamp was his only companion on the islands and he did not want to lose him. He discovered that he had even a certain affection for him. Next day he went to see the missionary.

"What's this I hear about your sister marrying Ginger Ted?" he asked him. "It's the most extraordinary thing I've ever heard in my life."

"It's true nevertheless."

"You must do something about it. It's madness."

"My sister is of full age and entitled to do as she pleases."

"But you don't mean to tell me you approve of it. You know Ginger Ted. He's a bum and there are no two ways about it. Have you told her the risk she's running? I mean, bringing sinners to repentance and all that sort of thing's all right, but there are limits. And does the leopard ever change his spots?"

Then for the first time in his life the Contrôleur saw a twinkle in the missionary's eye.

"My sister is a very determined woman, Mr. Gruyter," he replied. "From that night they spent on the island he never had a chance."

The Contrôleur gasped. He was as surprised as the prophet when the Lord opened the mouth of the ass, and she said unto Balaam, What have I done unto thee, that thou hast smitten me these three times? Perhaps Mr. Jones was human after all.

"*Allejesus!*" muttered the Contrôleur.

Before anything more could be said Miss Jones swept into the room. She was radiant. She looked ten years younger. Her cheeks were flushed and her nose was hardly red at all.

"Have you come to congratulate me, Mr. Gruyter?"

she cried, and her manner was sprightly and girlish. "You see, I was right after all. Everyone has some good in them. You don't know how splendid Edward has been all through this terrible time. He's a hero. He's a saint. Even I was surprised."

"I hope you'll be very happy, Miss Jones."

"I know I shall. Oh, it would be wicked of me to doubt it. For it is the Lord who has brought us together."

"Do you think so?"

"I know it. Don't you see? Except for the cholera Edward would never have found himself. Except for the cholera we should never have learnt to know one another. I have never seen the hand of God more plainly manifest."

The Contrôleur could not but think that it was rather a clumsy device to bring those two together that necessitated the death of six hundred innocent persons, but not being well versed in the ways of omnipotence he made no remark.

"You'll never guess where we're going for our honeymoon," said Miss Jones, perhaps a trifle archly.

"Java?"

"No, if you'll lend us the launch, we're going to that island where we were marooned. It has very tender recollections for both of us. It was there that I first guessed how fine and good Edward was. It's there I want him to have his reward."

The Contrôleur caught his breath. He left quickly, for he thought that unless he had a bottle of beer at once he would have a fit.

The Force of Circumstance

SHE was sitting on the verandah waiting for her husband to come in for luncheon. The Malay boy had drawn the blinds when the morning lost its freshness, but she had partly raised one of them so that she could look at the river. Under the breathless sun of midday it had the white pallor of death. A native was paddling along in a dug-out so small that it hardly showed above the surface of the water. The colours of the day were ashy and wan. They were but the various tones of the heat. (It was like an Eastern melody, in the minor key, which exacerbates the nerves by its ambiguous monotony; and the ear awaits impatiently a resolution, but waits in vain.) The cicadas sang their grating song with a frenzied energy; it was as continual and monotonous as the rustling of a brook over the stones; but on a sudden it was drowned by the loud singing of a bird, mellifluous and rich; and for an instant, with a catch at her heart, she thought of the English blackbird.

Then she heard her husband's step on the gravel path behind the bungalow, the path that led to the court-house in which he had been working, and she rose from her chair to greet him. He ran up the short flight of steps, for the bungalow was built on piles, and at the door the boy was waiting to take his topee. He came into the room which served them as a dining-room and parlour, and his eyes lit up with pleasure as he saw her.

"Hulloa, Doris. Hungry?"

"Ravenous."

"It'll only take me a minute to have a bath and then I'm ready."

"Be quick," she smiled.

He disappeared into his dressing-room and she heard him whistling cheerily while, with the carelessness with which she was always remonstrating, he tore off his clothes and flung them on the floor. He was twenty-nine, but he was still a schoolboy; he would never grow up. That was why she had fallen in love with him, perhaps, for no amount of affection could persuade her that he was good-looking. He was a little round man, with a red face like the full moon, and blue eyes. He was rather pimply. She had examined him carefully and had been forced to confess to him that he had not a single feature which she could praise. She had told him often that he wasn't her type at all.

"I never said I was a beauty," he laughed.

"I can't think what it is I see in you."

But of course she knew perfectly well. He was a gay, jolly little man, who took nothing very solemnly, and he was constantly laughing. He made her laugh too. He found life an amusing rather than a serious business, and he had a charming smile. When she was with him she felt happy and good-tempered. And the deep affection which she saw in those merry blue eyes of his touched her. It was very satisfactory to be loved like that. Once, sitting on his knees, during their honeymoon she had taken his face in her hands and said to him:

"You're an ugly, little fat man, Guy, but you've got charm. I can't help loving you."

A wave of emotion swept over her and her eyes filled with tears. She saw his face contorted for a moment with the extremity of his feeling and his voice was a little shaky when he answered.

"It's a terrible thing for me to have married a woman who's mentally deficient," he said.

She chuckled. It was the characteristic answer which she would have liked him to make.

It was hard to realise that nine months ago she had

never even heard of him. She had met him at a small place by the seaside where she was spending a month's holiday with her mother. Doris was secretary to a member of parliament. Guy was home on leave. They were staying at the same hotel, and he quickly told her all about himself. He was born in Sembulu, where his father had served for thirty years under the second Sultan, and on leaving school he had entered the same service. He was devoted to the country.

"After all, England's a foreign land to me," he told her. "My home's Sembulu."

And now it was her home too. He asked her to marry him at the end of the month's holiday. She had known he was going to, and had decided to refuse him. She was her widowed mother's only child and she could not go so far away from her, but when the moment came she did not quite know what happened to her, she was carried off her feet by an unexpected emotion, and she accepted him. They had been settled now for four months in the little outstation of which he was in charge. She was very happy.

She told him once that she had quite made up her mind to refuse him.

"Are you sorry you didn't?" he asked, with a merry smile in his twinkling blue eyes.

"I should have been a perfect fool if I had. What a bit of luck that fate or chance or whatever it was stepped in and took the matter entirely out of my hands!"

Now she heard Guy clatter down the steps to the bath-house. He was a noisy fellow and even with bare feet he could not be quiet. But he uttered an exclamation. He said two or three words in the local dialect and she could not understand. Then she heard someone speaking to him, not aloud, but in a sibilant whisper. Really it was too bad of people to waylay him when he was going to have his bath. He spoke again and though his voice was low she could hear that he was vexed. The other voice was raised now; it was a woman's. Doris supposed it was someone who had a complaint to make. It was like a Malay woman to come in that surreptitious way. But she was evidently getting very little from Guy, for she heard him say: Get out. That at all events she understood, and then she heard him bolt the door. There was a sound of the water he was throwing over himself (the bathing arrangements still amused her, the bath-houses were under the bedrooms, on the ground; you had a large tub of water and you sluiced yourself with a little tin pail) and in a couple of minutes he was back again in the dining-room. His hair was still wet. They sat down to luncheon.

"It's lucky I'm not a suspicious or a jealous person," she laughed. "I don't know that I should altogether approve of your having animated conversations with ladies while you're having your bath."

His face, usually so cheerful, had borne a sullen look when he came in, but now it brightened.

"I wasn't exactly pleased to see her."

"So I judged by the tone of your voice. In fact, I thought you were rather short with the young person."

"Damned cheek, waylaying me like that!"

"What did she want?"

"Oh, I don't know. It's a woman from the kampong. She's had a row with her husband or something."

"I wonder if it's the same one who was hanging about this morning."

He frowned a little.

"Was there someone hanging about?"

"Yes, I went into your dressing-room to see that everything was nice and tidy, and then I went down to the bath-house. I saw someone slink out of the door as I went down the steps and when I looked out I saw a woman standing there."

"Did you speak to her?"

"I asked her what she wanted and she said something,

but I couldn't understand."

"I'm not going to have all sorts of stray people prowling about here," he said. "They've got no right to come."

He smiled, but Doris, with the quick perception of a woman in love, noticed that he smiled only with his lips, not as usual with his eyes also, and wondered what it was that troubled him.

"What have you been doing this morning?" he asked.

"Oh, nothing much. I went for a little walk."

"Through the kampong?"

"Yes. I saw a man send a chained monkey up a tree to pick coconuts, which rather thrilled me."

"It's rather a lark, isn't it?"

"Oh, Guy, there were two little boys watching him who were much whiter than the others. I wondered if they were half-castes. I spoke to them, but they didn't know a word of English."

"There are two or three half-caste children in the kampong," he answered.

"Who do they belong to?"

"Their mother is one of the village girls."

"Who is their father?"

"Oh, my dear, that's the sort of question we think it a little dangerous to ask out here." He paused. "A lot of fellows have native wives, and then when they go home or marry they pension them off and send them back to their village."

Doris was silent. The indifference with which he spoke seemed a little callous to her. There was almost a frown on her frank, open, pretty English face when she replied.

"But what about the children?"

"I have no doubt they're properly provided for. Within his means, a man generally sees that there's enough money to have them decently educated. They get jobs as clerks in a government office, you know; they're all right."

She gave him a slightly rueful smile.

"You can't expect me to think it's a very good system."

"You mustn't be too hard," he smiled back.

"I'm not hard. But I'm thankful you never had a Malay wife. I should have hated it. Just think if those two little brats were yours."

The boy changed their plates. There was never much variety in their menu. They started luncheon with river fish, dull and insipid, so that a good deal of tomato ketchup was needed to make it palatable, and then went on to some kind of stew. Guy poured Worcester Sauce over it.

"The old Sultan didn't think it was a white woman's country," he said presently. "He rather encouraged people to – keep house with native girls. Of course things have changed now. The country's perfectly quiet and I suppose we know better how to cope with the climate."

"But, Guy, the eldest of those boys wasn't more than seven or eight and the other was about five."

"It's awfully lonely on an outstation. Why, often one doesn't see another white man for six months on end. A fellow comes out here when he's only a boy." He gave her that charming smile of his which transfigured his round, plain, face. "There are excuses, you know."

She always found that smile irresistible. It was his best argument. Her eyes grew once more soft and tender.

"I'm sure there are." She stretched her hand across the little table and put it on his. "I'm very lucky to have caught you so young. Honestly, it would upset me dreadfully if I were told that you had lived like that."

He took her hand and pressed it.

"Are you happy here, darling?"

"Desperately."

She looked very cool and fresh in her linen frock. The heat did not distress her. She had no more than the prettiness of youth, though her brown eyes were fine;

but she had a pleasing frankness of expression, and her dark, short hair was neat and glossy. She gave you the impression of a girl of spirit and you felt sure that the member of parliament for whom she worked had in her a very competent secretary.

"I loved the country at once," she said. "Although I'm alone so much I don't think I've ever once felt lonely."

Of course she had read novels about the Malay Archipelago and she had formed an impression of a sombre land with great ominous rivers and a silent, impenetrable jungle. When the little coasting steamer set them down at the mouth of the river, where a large boat, manned by a dozen Dyaks, was waiting to take them to the station, her breath was taken away by the beauty, friendly rather than awe-inspiring, of the scene. It had a gaiety, like the joyful singing of birds in the trees, which she had never expected. On each bank of the river were mangroves and nipah palms, and behind them the dense green of the forest. In the distance stretched blue mountains, range upon range, as far as the eye could see. She had no sense of confinement nor of gloom, but rather of openness and wide spaces where the exultant fancy could wander with delight. The green glittered in the sunshine and the sky was blithe and cheerful. The gracious land seemed to offer her a smiling welcome.

They rowed on, hugging a bank, and high overhead flew a pair of doves. A flash of colour, like a living jewel, dashed across their path. It was a kingfisher. Two monkeys, with their dangling tails, sat side by side on a branch. On the horizon, over there on the other side of the broad and turbid river, beyond the jungle, was a row of little white clouds, the only clouds in the sky, and they looked like a row of ballet-girls, dressed in white, waiting at the back of the stage, alert and merry, for the curtain to go up. Her heart was filled with joy; and now, remembering it all, her eyes rested on her husband with a grateful, assured affection.

And what fun it had been to arrange their living-room! It was very big. On the floor, when she arrived, was a torn and dirty matting; on the walls of unpainted wood hung (much too high up) photogravures of Academy pictures, Dyak shields and parangs. The tables were covered with Dyak cloth in sombre colours, and on them stood pieces of Brunei brass-ware, much in need of cleaning, empty cigarette tins and bits of Malay silver. There was a rough wooden shelf with cheap editions of novels and a number of old travel books in battered leather; and another shelf was crowded with empty bottles. It was a bachelor's room, untidy but stiff; and though it amused her she found it intolerably pathetic. It was a dreary, comfortless life that Guy had led there, and she threw her arms round his neck and kissed him.

"You poor darling," she laughed.

She had deft hands and she soon made the room habitable. She arranged this and that, and what she could not do with she turned out. Her wedding-presents helped. Now the room was friendly and comfortable. In glass vases were lovely orchids and in great bowls huge masses of flowering shrubs. She felt an inordinate pride because it was her house (she had never in her life lived in anything but a poky flat) and she had made it charming for him.

"Are you pleased with me?" she asked when she had finished.

"Quite," he smiled.

The deliberate understatement was much to her mind. How jolly it was that they should understand each other so well! They were both of them shy of displaying emotion, and it was only at rare moments that they used with one another anything but ironic banter.

They finished luncheon and he threw himself into a long chair to have a sleep. She went towards her room. She was a little surprised that he drew her to him as she passed and, making her bend down, kissed her lips. They were not in the habit of exchanging embraces at odd hours of the day.

"A full tummy is making you sentimental, my poor lamb," she chaffed him.

"Get out and don't let me see you again for at least two hours."

"Don't snore."

She left him. They had risen at dawn and in five minutes were fast asleep.

Doris was awakened by the sound of her husband's splashing in the bath-house. The walls of the bungalow were like a sounding-board and not a thing that one of them did escaped the other. She felt too lazy to move, but she heard the boy bring the tea things in, so she jumped up and ran down into her own bath-house. The water, not cold but cool, was deliciously refreshing. When she came into the sitting-room Guy was taking the rackets out of the press, for they played tennis in the short cool of the evening. The night fell at six.

The tennis-court was two or three hundred yards from the bungalow and after tea, anxious not to lose time, they strolled down to it.

"Oh, look," said Doris, "there's that girl that I saw this morning."

Guy turned quickly. His eyes rested for a moment on a native woman, but he did not speak.

"What a pretty sarong she's got," said Doris. "I wonder where it comes from."

They passed her. She was slight and small, with the large, dark, starry eyes of her race and a mass of raven hair. She did not stir as they went by, but stared at them strangely. Doris saw then that she was not quite so young as she had at first thought. Her features were a trifle heavy and her skin was dark, but she was very pretty. She held a small child in her arms. Doris smiled a little as she saw it, but no answering smile moved the woman's lips. Her face remained impassive. She did not look at Guy, she looked only at Doris, and he walked on as though he did not see her. Doris turned to him.

"Isn't that baby a duck?"

"I didn't notice."

She was puzzled by the look of his face. It was deathly white, and the pimples which not a little distressed her were more than commonly red.

"Did you notice her hands and feet? She might be a duchess."

"All natives have good hands and feet," he answered, but not jovially as was his wont; it was as though he forced himself to speak.

But Doris was not intrigued.

"Who is she, d'you know?"

"She's one of the girls in the kampong."

They had reached the court now. When Guy went up to the net to see that it was taut he looked back. The girl was still standing where they had passed her. Their eyes met.

"Shall I serve?" said Doris.

"Yes, you've got the balls on your side."

He played very badly. Generally he gave her fifteen and beat her, but to-day she won easily. And he played silently. Generally he was a noisy player, shouting all the time, cursing his foolishness when he missed a ball and chaffing her when he placed one out of her reach.

"You're off your game, young man," she cried.

"Not a bit," he said.

He began to slam the balls, trying to beat her, and sent one after the other into the net. She had never seen him with that set face. Was it possible that he was a little out of temper because he was not playing well? The light fell, and they ceased to play. The woman whom they had passed stood in exactly the same position as when they came and once more, with expressionless face, she watched them go.

The blinds on the verandah were raised now and on the table between their two long chairs were bottles and soda-water. This was the hour at which they had the first drink of the day and Guy mixed a couple of gin slings. The river stretched widely before them and on the further bank the jungle was wrapped in the mystery of the approaching night. A native was silently rowing up-stream, standing at the bow of the boat, with two oars.

"I played like a fool," said Guy, breaking a silence. "I'm feeling a bit under the weather."

"I'm sorry. You're not going to have fever, are you?"

"Oh, no. I shall be all right to-morrow."

Darkness closed in upon them. The frogs croaked loudly and now and then they heard a few short notes from some singing bird of the night. Fireflies flitted across the verandah and they made the trees that surrounded it look like Christmas trees lit with tiny candles. They sparkled softly. Doris thought she heard a little sigh. It vaguely disturbed her. Guy was always so full of gaiety.

"What is it, old man?" she said gently. "Tell mother."

"Nothing. Time for another drink," he answered breezily.

Next day he was as cheerful as ever and the mail came. The coasting steamer passed the mouth of the river twice a month, once on its way to the coalfields and once on its way back. On the outward journey it brought mail, which Guy sent a boat down to fetch. Its arrival was the excitement of their uneventful lives. For the first day or two they skimmed rapidly all that had come, letters, English papers and papers from Singapore, magazines and books, leaving for the ensuing weeks a more exact perusal. They snatched the illustrated papers from one another. If Doris had not been so absorbed she might have noticed that there was a change in Guy. She would have found it hard to describe and harder still to explain. There was in his eyes a sort of watchfulness and in his mouth a slight droop of anxiety.

Then, perhaps a week later, one morning when she was sitting in the shaded room studying a Malay grammar (for she was industriously learning the language) she heard a commotion in the compound. She heard the house boy's voice, he was speaking angrily, the voice of another man, perhaps it was the water-carrier's, and then a woman's, shrill and vituperative. There was a scuffle. She went to the window and opened the shutters. The water-carrier had hold of a woman's arm and was dragging her along, while the house boy was pushing her from behind with both hands. Doris recognised her at once as the woman she had seen one morning loitering in the compound and later in the day outside the tennis-court. She was holding a baby against her breast. All three were shouting angrily.

"Stop," cried Doris. "What are you doing?"

At the sound of her voice the water-carrier let go suddenly and the woman, still pushed from behind, fell to the ground. There was a sudden silence and the house boy looked sullenly into space. The water-carrier hesitated a moment and then slunk away. The woman raised herself slowly to her feet, arranged the baby on her arm, and stood impassive, staring at Doris. The boy said something to her which Doris could not have heard even if she had understood; the woman by no change of face showed that his words meant anything to her; but she slowly strolled away. The boy followed her to the gate of the compound. Doris called to him as he walked back, but he pretended not to hear. She was growing angry now and she called more sharply.

"Come here at once," she cried.

Suddenly, avoiding her wrathful glance, he came towards the bungalow. He came in and stood at the door. He looked at her sulkily.

"What were you doing with that woman?" she

asked abruptly.

"Tuan say she no come here."

"You mustn't treat a woman like that. I won't have it. I shall tell the tuan exactly what I saw."

The boy did not answer. He looked away, but she felt that he was watching her through his long eyelashes. She dismissed him.

"That'll do."

Without a word he turned and went back to the servants' quarters. She was exasperated and she found it impossible to give her attention once more to the Malay exercises. In a little while the boy came in to lay the cloth for luncheon. On a sudden he went to the door.

"What is it?" she asked.

"Tuan just coming."

He went out to take Guy's hat from him. His quick ears had caught the footsteps before they were audible to her. Guy did not as usual come up the steps immediately; he paused, and Doris at once surmised that the boy had gone down to meet him in order to tell him of the morning's incident. She shrugged her shoulders. The boy evidently wanted to get his story in first. But she was astonished when Guy came in. His face was ashy.

"Guy, what on earth's the matter?"

He flushed a sudden hot red.

"Nothing. Why?"

She was so taken aback that she let him pass into his room without a word of what she had meant to speak of at once. It took him longer than usual to have his bath and change his clothes and luncheon was served when he came in.

"Guy," she said, as they sat down, "that woman we saw the other day was here again this morning"

"So I've heard," he answered.

"The boys were treating her brutally. I had to stop them. You must really speak to them about it."

Though the Malay understood every word she said, he made no sign that he heard. He handed her the toast.

"She's been told not to come here. I gave instructions that if she showed herself again she was to be turned out."

"Were they obliged to be so rough?"

"She refused to go. I don't think they were any rougher than they could help."

"It was horrible to see a woman treated like that. She had a baby in her arms."

"Hardly a baby. It's three years old."

"How d'you know?"

"I know all about her. She hasn't the least right to come here pestering everybody."

"What does she want?"

"She wants to do exactly what she did. She wants to make a disturbance."

For a little while Doris did not speak. She was surprised at her husband's tone. He spoke tersely. He spoke as though all this were no concern of hers. She thought him a little unkind. He was nervous and irritable.

"I doubt if we shall be able to play tennis this afternoon," he said. "It looks to me as though we were going to have a storm."

The rain was falling when she awoke and it was impossible to go out. During tea Guy was silent and abstracted. She got her sewing and began to work. Guy sat down to read such of the English papers as he had not yet gone through from cover to cover; but he was restless; he walked up and down the large room and then went out on the verandah. He looked at the steady rain. What was he thinking of? Doris was vaguely uneasy.

It was not till after dinner that he spoke. During the simple meal he had exerted himself to be his usual gay self, but the exertion was apparent. The rain had ceased and the night was starry. They sat on the verandah. In order not to attract insects they had put out the lamp in the sitting-room. At their feet, with a mighty, formidable sluggishness, silent, mysterious and fatal, flowed the river. It had the terrible deliberation and the relentlessness of destiny.

"Doris, I've got something to say to you," he said suddenly.

His voice was very strange. Was it her fancy that he had difficulty in keeping it quite steady? She felt a little pang in her heart because he was in distress, and she put her hand gently into his. He drew it away.

"It's rather a long story. I'm afraid it's not a very nice one and I find it rather difficult to tell. I'm going to ask you not to interrupt me, or to say anything, till I've finished."

In the darkness she could not see his face, but she felt that it was haggard. She did not answer. He spoke in a voice so low that it hardly broke the silence of the night.

"I was only eighteen when I came out here. I came straight from school. I spent three months in Kuala Solor, and then I was sent to a station up the Sembulu river. Of course there was a Resident there and his wife. I lived in the court-house, but I used to have my meals with them and spend the evening with them. I had an awfully good time. Then the fellow who was here fell ill and had to go home. We were short of men on account of the war and I was put in charge of this place. Of course I was very young, but I spoke the language like a native, and they remembered my father. I was as pleased as punch to be on my own."

He was silent while he knocked the ashes out of his pipe and refilled it. When he lit a match Doris, without looking at him, noticed that his hand was unsteady.

"I'd never been alone before. Of course at home there'd been father and mother and generally an assistant. And then at school naturally there were always fellows about. On the way out, on the boat, there were people all the time, and at K.S., and the same at my first post. The people there were almost like my own people. I seemed always to live in a crowd. I like people. I'm a noisy blighter. I like to have a good time. All sorts of things make me laugh and you must have somebody to laugh with. But it was different here. Of course it was all right in the day time; I had my work and I could talk to the Dyaks. Although they were head-hunters in those days and now and then I had a bit of trouble with them, they were an awfully decent lot of fellows. I got on very well with them. Of course I should have liked a white man to gas to, but they were better than nothing, and it was easier for me because they didn't look upon me quite as a stranger. I liked the work too. It was rather lonely in the evening to sit on the verandah and drink a gin and bitters by myself, but I could read. And the boys were about. My own boy was called Abdul. He'd known my father. When I got tired of reading I could give him a shout and have a bit of a jaw with him.

"It was the nights that did for me. After dinner the boys shut up and went away to sleep in the kampong. I was all alone. There wasn't a sound in the bungalow except now and then the croak of the chik-chak. It used to come out of the silence, suddenly, so that it made me jump. Over in the kampong I heard the sound of a gong or fire-crackers. They were having a good time, they weren't so far away, but I had to stay where I was. I was tired of reading. I couldn't have been more of a prisoner if I'd been in jail. Night after night it was the same. I tried drinking three or four whiskies, but it's poor fun drinking alone, and it didn't cheer me up; it only made me feel rather rotten next day. I tried going to bed immediately after dinner, but I couldn't sleep. I used to lie in bed, getting hotter and hotter, and more wide awake, till I didn't know what to do with myself. By George, those nights were long. D'you know, I got so low, I was so sorry for myself that sometimes – it makes me laugh now when I think of it, but I was only nineteen and a half – sometimes I used to cry.

"Then, one evening, after dinner, Abdul had cleared away and was just going off, when he gave a little cough. He said, wasn't I lonely in the house all night by myself? 'Oh, no, that's all right,' I said. I didn't want him to know what a damned fool I was, but I expect he knew all right. He stood there without speaking, and I knew he wanted to say something to me. 'What is it?' I said. 'Spit it out.' Then he said that if I'd like to have a girl to come and live with me he knew one who was willing. She was a very good girl and he could recommend her. She'd be no trouble and it would be someone to have about the bungalow. She'd mend my things for me.... I felt awfully low. It had been raining all day and I hadn't been able to get any exercise. I knew I shouldn't sleep for hours. It wouldn't cost me very much money, he said, her people were poor and they'd be quite satisfied with a small present. Two hundred Straits dollars. 'You look,' he said. 'If you don't like her you send her away.' I asked him where she was. 'She's here,' he said. 'I call her.' He went to the door. She'd been waiting on the steps with her mother. They came in and sat down on the floor. I gave them some sweets. She was shy, of course, but cool enough, and when I said something to her she gave me a smile. She was very young, hardly more than a child, they said she was fifteen. She was awfully pretty, and she had her best clothes on. We began to talk. She didn't say much, but she laughed a lot when I chaffed her. Abdul said I'd find she had plenty to say for herself when she got to know me. He told her to come and sit by me. She giggled and refused, but her mother told her to come, and I made room for her on the chair. She blushed and laughed, but she came, and then she snuggled up to me. The boy laughed too. 'You see, she's taken to you already,' he said. 'Do you want her to stay?' he asked. 'Do you want to?' I said to her. She hid her face, laughing, on my shoulder. She was very soft and small. 'Very well,' I said, 'let her stay.' "

Guy leaned forward and helped himself to a whisky and soda.

"May I speak now?" asked Doris.

"Wait a minute, I haven't finished yet. I wasn't in love with her, not even at the beginning. I only took her so as to have somebody about the bungalow. I think I should have gone mad if I hadn't, or else taken to drink. I was at the end of my tether. I was too young to be quite alone. I was never in love with anyone but you." He hesitated a moment. "She lived here till I went home last year on leave. It's the woman you've seen hanging about."

"Yes, I guessed that. She had a baby in her arms. Is that your child?"

"Yes. It's a little girl."

"Is it the only one?"

"You saw the two small boys the other day in the kampong. You mentioned them."

"She has three children then?"

"Yes."

"It's quite a family you've got."

She felt the sudden gesture which her remark forced from him, but he did not speak.

"Didn't she know that you were married till you suddenly turned up here with a wife?" asked Doris.

"She knew I was going to be married."

"When?"

"I sent her back to the village before I left here. I told her it was all over. I gave her what I'd promised. She always knew it was only a temporary arrangement. I was fed up with it. I told her I was going to marry a white woman."

"But you hadn't even seen me then."

"No, I know. But I'd made up my mind to marry when I was home." He chuckled in his old manner. "I don't mind telling you that I was getting rather despondent about it when I met you. I fell in love with you at first sight and then I knew it was either you or nobody."

"Why didn't you tell me? Don't you think it would have been only fair to give me a chance of judging for myself? It might have occurred to you that it would be rather a shock to a girl to find out that her husband had lived for ten years with another girl and had three children."

"I couldn't expect you to understand. The circumstances out here are peculiar. It's the regular thing. Five men out of six do it. I thought perhaps it would shock you and I didn't want to lose you. You see, I was most awfully in love with you. I am now, darling. There was no reason that you should ever know. I didn't expect to come back here. One seldom goes back to the same station after home leave. When we came here I offered her money if she'd go to some other village. first she said she would and then she changed her mind."

"Why have you told me now?"

"She's been making the most awful scenes. I don't know how she found out that you knew nothing about it. As soon as she did she began to blackmail me. I've had to give her an awful lot of money. I gave orders that she wasn't to be allowed in the compound. This morning she made that scene just to attract your attention. She wanted to frighten me. It couldn't go on like that. I thought the only thing was to make a clean breast of it."

There was a long silence as he finished. At last he put his hand on hers.

"You do understand, Doris, don't you? I know I've been to blame."

She did not move her hand. He felt it cold beneath his.

"Is she jealous?"

"I daresay there were all sorts of perks when she was living here, and I don't suppose she much likes not getting them any longer. But she was never in love with me any more than I was in love with her. Native women never do really care for white men, you know."

"And the children?"

"Oh, the children are all right. I've provided for them. As soon as the boys are old enough I shall send them to school at Singapore."

"Do they mean nothing to you at all?"

He hesitated.

"I want to be quite frank with you. I should be sorry if anything happened to them. When the first one was expected I thought I'd be much fonder of it than I ever had been of its mother. I suppose I should have been if it had been white. Of course, when it was a baby it was rather funny and touching, but I had no particular feeling that it was mine. I think that's what it is; you see, I have no sense of their belonging to me. I've reproached myself sometimes, because it seemed rather unnatural, but the honest truth is that they're no more to me than if they were somebody else's children. Of course a lot of slush is talked about children by people who haven't got any."

Now she had heard everything. He waited for her to speak, but she said nothing. She sat motionless.

"Is there anything more you want to ask me, Doris?" he said at last.

"No, I've got rather a headache. I think I shall go to bed." Her voice was as steady as ever. "I don't quite know what to say. Of course it's been all very unexpected. You must give me a little time to think."

"Are you very angry with me?"

"No. Not at all. Only – only I must be left to myself for a while. Don't move. I'm going to bed."

She rose from her long chair and put her hand on his shoulder.

"It's so very hot to-night. I wish you'd sleep in your dressing-room. Good-night."

She was gone. He heard her lock the door of her bedroom.

She was pale next day and he could see that she had not slept. There was no bitterness in her manner, she talked as usual, but without ease; she spoke of this and that as though she were making conversation with a stranger. They had never had a quarrel, but it seemed to Guy that so would she talk if they had had a disagreement and the subsequent reconciliation had left her still wounded. The look in her eyes puzzled him; he seemed to read in them a strange fear. Immediately after dinner she said:

"I'm not feeling very well to-night. I think I shall go straight to bed."

"Oh, my poor darling, I'm so sorry," he cried.

"It's nothing. I shall be all right in a day or two."

"I shall come in and say good-night to you later."

"No, don't do that. I shall try and get straight off to sleep."

"Well, then, kiss me before you go."

He saw that she flushed. For an instant she seemed to hesitate; then, with averted eyes, she leaned towards him. He took her in his arms and sought her lips, but she turned her face away and he kissed her cheek. She left him quickly and again he heard the key turn softly in the lock of her door. He flung himself heavily on the chair. He tried to read, but his ear was attentive to the smallest sound in his wife's room. She had said she was going to bed, but he did not hear her move. The silence in there made him unaccountably nervous. Shading the lamp with his hand he saw that there was a glimmer under her door; she had not put out her light. What on earth was she doing? He put down his book. It would not have surprised him if she had been angry and had made him a scene, or if she had cried; he could have coped with that; but her calmness frightened him. And then what was that fear which he had seen so plainly in her eyes? He thought once more over all he had said to her on the previous night. He didn't know how else he could have put it. After all, the chief point was that he'd done the same as everybody else, and it was all over long before he met her. Of course as things turned out he had been a fool, but anyone could be wise after the event. He put his hand to his heart. Funny how it hurt him there.

"I suppose that's the sort of thing people mean when they say they're heartbroken," he said to himself. "I wonder how long it's going on like this?"

Should he knock at the door and tell her he must speak to her? It was better to have it out. He *must* make her understand. But the silence scared him. Not a sound! Perhaps it was better to leave her alone. Of course it had been a shock. He must give her as long as she wanted. After all, she knew how devotedly he loved her. Patience, that was the only thing; perhaps she was fighting it out with herself; he must give her time; he must have patience.

Next morning he asked her if she had slept better.

"Yes, much," she said.

"Are you very angry with me?" he asked piteously.

She looked at him with candid, open eyes.

"Not a bit."

"Oh, my dear, I'm so glad. I've been a brute and a beast. I know it's been hateful for you. But do forgive me. I've been so miserable."

"I do forgive you. I don't even blame you."

He gave her a little rueful smile, and there was in his eyes the look of a whipped dog.

"I haven't much liked sleeping by myself the last two nights."

She glanced away. Her face grew a trifle paler.

"I've had the bed in my room taken away. It took up so much space. I've had a little camp bed put there instead."

"My dear, what are you talking about?"

Now she looked at him steadily.

"I'm not going to live with you as your wife again."

"Never?"

She shook her head. He looked at her in a puzzled way. He could hardly believe he had heard aright and his heart began to beat painfully.

"But that's awfully unfair to me, Doris."

"Don't you think it was a little unfair to me to bring me out here in the circumstances?"

"But you just said you didn't blame me."

"That's quite true. But the other's different. I can't do it."

"But how are we going to live together like that?"

She stared at the floor. She seemed to ponder deeply.

"When you wanted to kiss me on the lips last night I – it almost made me sick."

"Doris."

She looked at him suddenly and her eyes were cold and hostile.

"That bed I slept on, is that the bed in which she had her children?" She saw him flush deeply. "Oh, it's horrible. How could you?" She wrung her hands, and her twisting, tortured fingers looked like little writhing snakes. But she made a great effort and controlled herself. "My mind is quite made up. I don't want to be unkind to you, but there are some things that you can't ask me to do. I've thought it all over. I've been thinking of nothing else since you told me, night and day, till I'm exhausted. My first instinct was to get up and go. At once. The steamer will be here in two or three days."

"Doesn't it mean anything to you that I love you?"

"Oh, I know you love me. I'm not going to do that. I want to give us both a chance. I have loved you so, Guy." Her voice broke, but she did not cry. "I don't want to be unreasonable. Heaven knows, I don't want to be unkind. Guy, will you give me time?"

"I don't know quite what you mean."

"I just want you to leave me alone. I'm frightened by the feelings that I have."

He had been right then; she was afraid.

"What feelings?"

"Please don't ask me. I don't want to say anything to wound you. Perhaps I shall get over them. Heaven knows, I want to. I'll try, I promise you. I'll try. Give me six months. I'll do everything in the world for you, but just that one thing." She made a little gesture of appeal. "There's no reason why we shouldn't be happy enough together. If you really love me you'll – you'll have patience."

He sighed deeply.

"Very well," he said. "Naturally I don't want to force you to do anything you don't like. It shall be as you say."

He sat heavily for a little, as though, on a sudden grown old, it was an effort to move; then he got up. "I'll be getting along to the office."

He took his topee and went out.

A month passed. Women conceal their feelings better than men and a stranger visiting them would never have guessed that Doris was in any way troubled. But in Guy the strain was obvious; his round, good-natured face was drawn, and in his eyes was a hungry, harassed look. He watched Doris. She was gay and she chaffed him as she had been used to do; they played tennis together; they chatted about one thing and another. But it was evident that she was merely playing a part, and at last, unable to contain himself, he tried to speak again of his connections with the Malay woman.

"Oh, Guy, there's no object in going back on all that," she answered breezily. "We've said all we had to say about it and I don't blame you for anything."

"Why do you punish me then?"

"My poor boy, I don't want to punish you. It's not my fault if..." she shrugged her shoulders. "Human nature is very odd."

"I don't understand."

"Don't try."

The words might have been harsh, but she softened them with a pleasant, friendly smile. Every night when she went to bed she leaned over Guy and lightly kissed his cheek. Her lips only touched it. It was as though a moth had just brushed his face in its flight.

A second month passed, then a third, and suddenly the six months which had seemed so interminable were over. Guy asked himself whether she remembered. He gave a strained attention now to everything she said, to every look on her face and to every gesture of her hands. She remained impenetrable. She had asked him to give her six months; well, he had.

The coasting steamer passed the mouth of the river, dropped their mail, and went on its way. Guy busily wrote the letters which it would pick up on the return journey. Two or three days passed by. It was a Tuesday and the prahu was to start at dawn on Thursday to await the steamer. Except at meal time when Doris exerted herself to make conversation they had not of late talked very much together; and after dinner as usual they took their books and began to read; but when the boy had finished clearing away and was gone for the night Doris put down hers.

"Guy, I have something I want to say to you," she murmured.

His heart gave a sudden thud against his ribs and he felt himself change colour.

"Oh, my dear, don't look like that, it's not so very

terrible," she laughed.

But he thought her voice trembled a little.

"Well?"

"I want you to do something for me."

"My darling, I'll do anything in the world for you."

He put out his hand to take hers, but she drew it away.

"I want you to let me go home."

"You?" he cried, aghast. "When? Why?"

"I've borne it as long as I can. I'm at the end of my tether."

"How long do you want to go for? For always?"

"I don't know. I think so." She gathered determination. "Yes, for always."

"Oh, my God!"

His voice broke and she thought he was going to cry.

"Oh, Guy, don't blame me. It really is not my fault. I can't help myself."

"You asked me for six months. I accepted your terms. You can't say I've made a nuisance of myself."

"No, no."

"I've tried not to let you see what a rotten time I was having."

"I know. I'm very grateful to you. You've been awfully kind to me. Listen, Guy, I want to tell you again that I don't blame you for a single thing you did. After all, you were only a boy, and you did no more than the others; I know what the loneliness is here. Oh, my dear, I'm so dreadfully sorry for you. I knew all that from the beginning. That's why I asked you for six months. My commonsense tells me that I'm making a mountain out of a molehill. I'm unreasonable; I'm being unfair to you. But, you see, commonsense has nothing to do with it; my whole soul is in revolt. When I see the woman and her children in the village I just feel my legs shaking. Everything in this house; when I think of that bed I slept in it gives me goose-flesh.... You don't know what I've endured."

"I think I've persuaded her to go away. And I've applied for a transfer."

"That wouldn't help. She'll be there always. You belong to them, you don't belong to me. I think perhaps I could have stood it if there'd only been one child, but three; and the boys are quite big boys. For ten years you lived with her." And now she came out with what she had been working up to. She was desperate. "It's a physical thing. I can't help it, it's stronger than I am. I think of those thin black arms of hers round you and it fills me with a physical nausea. I think of you holding those little black babies in your arms. Oh, it's loathsome. The touch of you is odious to me. Each night, when I've kissed you, I've had to brace myself up to it, I've had to clench my hands and force myself to touch your cheek." Now she was clasping and unclasping her fingers in a nervous agony, and her voice was out of control. "I know it's I who am to blame now. I'm a silly, hysterical woman. I thought I'd get over it. I can't, and now I never shall. I've brought it all on myself; I'm willing to take the consequences; if you say I must stay here, I'll stay, but if I stay I shall die. I beseech you to let me go."

And now the tears which she had restrained so long overflowed and she wept broken-heartedly. He had never seen her cry before.

"Of course I don't want to keep you here against your will," he said hoarsely.

Exhausted, she leaned back in her chair. Her features were all twisted and awry. It was horribly painful to see the abandonment of grief on that face which was habitually so placid.

"I'm so sorry, Guy. I've broken your life, but I've broken mine too. And we might have been so happy."

"When do you want to go? On Thursday?"

"Yes."

She looked at him piteously. He buried his face in his

hands. At last he looked up.

"I'm tired out," he muttered.

"May I go?"

"Yes."

For two minutes perhaps they sat there without a word. She started when the chik-chak gave its piercing, hoarse and strangely human cry. Guy rose and went out on to the verandah. He leaned against the rail and looked at the softly flowing water. He heard Doris go into her room.

Next morning, up earlier than usual, he went to her door and knocked.

"Yes?"

"I have to go up-river to-day. I shan't be back till late."

"All right."

She understood. He had arranged to be away all day in order not to be about while she was packing. It was heartbreaking work. When she had packed her clothes she looked round the sitting-room at the things that belonged to her. It seemed dreadful to take them. She left everything but the photograph of her mother. Guy did not come in till ten o'clock at night.

"I'm sorry I couldn't get back to dinner," he said. "The headman at the village I had to go to had a lot of things for me to attend to."

She saw his eyes wander about the room and notice that her mother's photograph no longer stood in its place.

"Is everything quite ready?" he asked. "I've ordered the boatman to be at the steps at dawn."

"I told the boy to wake me at five."

"I'd better give you some money." He went to his desk and wrote out a cheque. He took some notes from a drawer. "Here's some cash to take you as far as Singapore and at Singapore you'll be able to change the cheque."

"Thank you."

"Would you like me to come to the mouth of the river with you?"

"Oh, I think it would be better if we said good-bye here."

"All right. I think I shall turn in. I've had a long day and I'm dead beat."

He did not even touch her hand. He went into his room. In a few minutes she heard him throw himself on his bed. For a little while she sat looking for the last time round that room in which she had been so happy and so miserable. She sighed deeply. She got up and went into her own room. Everything was packed except the one or two things she needed for the night.

It was dark when the boy awakened them. They dressed hurriedly and when they were ready breakfast was waiting for them. Presently they heard the boat row up to the landing-stage below the bungalow, and then the servants carried down her luggage. It was a poor pretence they made of eating. The darkness thinned away and the river was ghostly. It was not yet day, but it was no longer night. In the silence the voices of the natives at the landing-stage were very clear. Guy glanced at his wife's untouched plate.

"If you've finished we might stroll down. I think you ought to be starting."

She did not answer. She rose from the table. She went into her room to see that nothing had been forgotten and then side by side with him walked down the steps. A little winding path led them to the river. At the landing-stage the native guards in their smart uniform were lined up and they presented arms as Guy and Doris passed. The head boatman gave her his hand as she stepped into the boat. She turned and looked at Guy. She wanted desperately to say one last word of comfort, once more to ask for his forgiveness, but she seemed to be struck dumb.

He stretched out his hand.

"Well, good-bye, I hope you'll have a jolly journey."

They shook hands.

Guy nodded to the head boatman and the boat pushed off. The dawn now was creeping along the river mistily, but the night lurked still in the dark trees of the jungle. He stood at the landing-stage till the boat was lost in the shadows of the morning. With a sigh he turned away. He nodded absent-mindedly when the guard once more presented arms. But when he reached the bungalow he called the boy. He went round the room picking out everything that had belonged to Doris.

"Pack all these things up," he said. "It's no good leaving them about."

Then he sat down on the verandah and watched the day advance gradually like a bitter, an unmerited and an overwhelming sorrow. At last he looked at his watch. It was time for him to go to the office.

In the afternoon he could not sleep, his head ached miserably, so he took his gun and went for a tramp in the jungle. He shot nothing, but he walked in order to tire himself out. Towards sunset he came back and had two or three drinks, and then it was time to dress for dinner. There wasn't much use in dressing now; he might just as well be comfortable; he put on a loose native jacket and a sarong. That was what he had been accustomed to wear before Doris came. He was barefoot. He ate his dinner listlessly and the boy cleared away and went. He sat down to read the *Tatler*. The bungalow was very silent. He could not read and let the paper fall on his knees. He was exhausted. He could not think and his mind was strangely vacant. The chik-chak was noisy that night and its hoarse and sudden cry seemed to mock him. You could hardly believe that this reverberating sound came from so small a throat. Presently he heard a discreet cough.

"Who' there?" he cried.

There was a pause. He looked at the door. The chik-chak laughed harshly. A small boy sidled in and stood on the threshold. It was a little half-caste boy in a tattered singlet and a sarong. It was the elder of his two sons.

"What do you want?" said Guy.

The boy came forward into the room and sat down, tucking his legs away under him.

"Who told you to come here?"

"My mother sent me. She says, do you want anything?"

Guy looked at the boy intently. The boy said nothing more. He sat and waited, his eyes cast down shyly. Then Guy in deep and bitter reflection buried his face in his hands. What was the use? It was finished. Finished! He surrendered. He sat back in his chair and sighed deeply.

"Tell your mother to pack up her things and yours. She can come back."

"When?" asked the boy, impassively.

Hot tears trickled down Guy's funny, round spotty face.

"To-night."

The Door of Opportunity

THEY got a first-class carriage to themselves. It was lucky, because they were taking a good deal in with them, Alban's suit-case and a hold-all, Anne's dressing-case and her hat-box. They had two trunks in the van, containing what they wanted immediately, but all the rest of their luggage Alban had put in the care of an agent who was to take it up to London and store it till they had made up their minds what to do. They had a lot, pictures and books, curios that Alban had collected in the East, his guns and saddles. They had left Sondurah for ever. Alban, as was his way, tipped the porter generously and then went to the bookstall and bought papers. He bought the *New Statesman* and the *Nation*, and the *Tatler* and the *Sketch*, and the last number of the *London Mercury*. He came back to the carriage and threw them on the seat.

"It's only an hour's journey," said Anne.

"I know, but I wanted to buy them. I've been starved so long. Isn't it grand to think that to-morrow morning we shall have to-morrow's *Times*, and the *Express* and the *Mail*?"

She did not answer and he turned away, for he saw coming towards them two persons, a man and his wife, who had been fellow-passengers from Singapore.

"Get through the Customs all right?" he cried to them cheerily.

The man seemed not to hear, for he walked straight on, but the woman answered.

"Yes, they never found the cigarettes."

She saw Anne, gave her a friendly little smile, and

passed on. Anne flushed.

"I was afraid they'd want to come in here," said Alban. "Let's have the carriage to ourselves if we can."

She looked at him curiously.

"I don't think you need worry," she answered. "I don't think anyone will come in."

He lit a cigarette and lingered at the carriage door. On his face was a happy smile. When they had passed through the Red Sea and found a sharp wind in the Canal, Anne had been surprised to see how much the men who had looked presentable enough in the white ducks in which she had been accustomed to see them, were changed when they left them off for warmer clothes. They looked like nothing on earth then. Their ties were awful and their shirts all wrong. They wore grubby flannel trousers and shabby old golf-coats that had too obviously been bought off the nail, or blue serge suits that betrayed the provincial tailor. Most of the passengers had got off at Marseilles, but a dozen or so, either because after a long period in the East they thought the trip through the Bay would do them good, or, like themselves, for economy's sake, had gone all the way to Tilbury, and now several of them walked along the platform. They wore solar topees or double-brimmed terais, and heavy greatcoats, or else shapeless soft hats or bowlers, not too well brushed, that looked too small for them. It was a shock to see them. They looked suburban and a trifle second-rate. But Alban had already a London look. There was not a speck of dust on his smart greatcoat, and his black Homburg hat looked brand-new. You would never have guessed that he had not been home for three years. His collar fitted closely round his neck and his foulard tie was neatly tied. As Anne looked at him she could not but think how good-looking he was. He was just under six feet tall, and slim, and he wore his clothes well, and his clothes were well cut. He had fair hair, still thick, and blue eyes and the faintly yellow skin common to men of that complexion after they have lost the pink-and-white freshness of early youth. There was no colour in his cheeks. It was a fine head, well-set on rather a long neck, with a somewhat prominent Adam's apple; but you were more impressed with the distinction than with the beauty of his face. It was because his features were so regular, his nose so straight, his brow so broad that he photographed so well. Indeed, from his photographs you would have thought him extremely handsome. He was not that, perhaps because his eyebrows and his eyelashes were pale, and his lips thin, but he looked very intellectual. There was refinement in his face and a spirituality that was oddly moving. That was how you thought a poet should look; and when Anne became engaged to him she told her girl friends who asked her about him that he looked like Shelley. He turned to her now with a little smile in his blue eyes. His smile was very attractive.

"What a perfect day to land in England!"

It was October. They had steamed up the Channel on a grey sea under a grey sky. There was not a breath of wind. The fishing boats seemed to rest on the placid water as though the elements had for ever forgotten their old hostility. The coast was incredibly green, but with a bright cosy greenness quite unlike the luxuriant, vehement verdure of Eastern jungles. The red towns they passed here and there were comfortable and homelike. They seemed to welcome the exiles with a smiling friendliness. And when they drew into the estuary of the Thames they saw the rich levels of Essex and in a little while Chalk Church on the Kentish shore, lonely in the midst of weather-beaten trees, and beyond it the woods of Cobham. The sun, red in a faint mist, set on the marshes, and night fell. In the station the arc-lamps shed a light that spotted the darkness with cold hard patches. It was good to see the porters lumbering about in their grubby uniforms and the stationmaster fat and important in his bowler hat. The stationmaster blew a whistle and waved his arm. Alban stepped into the carriage and seated himself in the corner opposite to Anne. The train started.

"We're due in London at six-ten," said Alban. "We ought to get to Jermyn Street by seven. That'll give us an hour to bath and change and we can get to the Savoy for dinner by eight-thirty. A bottle of pop to-night, my pet, and a slap-up dinner." He gave a chuckle. "I heard the Strouds and the Maundys arranging to meet at the Trocadero Grill-Room."

He took up the papers and asked if she wanted any of them. Anne shook her head.

"Tired?" he smiled.

"No."

"Excited?"

In order not to answer she gave a little laugh. He began to look at the papers, starting with the publishers' advertisements, and she was conscious of the intense satisfaction it was to him to feel himself through them once more in the middle of things. They had taken in those same papers in Sondurah, but they arrived six weeks old, and though they kept them abreast of what was going on in the world that interested them both, they emphasised their exile. But these were fresh from the press. They smelt different. They had a crispness that was almost voluptuous. He wanted to read them all at once. Anne looked out of the window. The country was dark, and she could see little but the lights of their carriage reflected on the glass, but very soon the town encroached upon it, and then she saw little sordid houses, mile upon mile of them, with a light in a window here and there, and the chimneys made a dreary pattern against the sky. They passed through Barking and East Ham and Bromley – it was silly that the name on the platform as they went through the station should give her such a tremor – and then Stepney. Alban put down his papers.

"We shall be there in five minutes now."

He put on his hat and took down from the racks the things the porter had put in them. He looked at her with shining eyes and his lips twitched. She saw that he was only just able to control his emotion. He looked out of the window, too, and they passed over brightly lighted thoroughfares, close packed with tram-cars, buses and motor-vans, and they saw the streets thick with people. What a mob! The shops were all lit up. They saw the hawkers with their barrows at the kerb.

"London," he said.

He took her hand and gently pressed it. His smile was so sweet that she had to say something. She tried to be facetious.

"Does it make you feel all funny inside?"

"I don't know if I want to cry or if I want to be sick."

Fenchurch Street. He lowered the window and waved his arm for a porter. With a grinding of brakes the train came to a standstill. A porter opened the door and Alban handed him out one package after another. Then in his polite way, having jumped out, he gave his hand to Anne to help her down to the platform. The porter went to fetch a barrow and they stood by the pile of their luggage. Alban waved to two passengers from the ship who passed them. The man nodded stiffly.

"What a comfort it is that we shall never have to be civil to those awful people any more," said Alban lightly.

Anne gave him a quick glance. He was really incomprehensible. The porter came back with his barrow, the luggage was put on and they followed him to collect their trunks. Alban took his wife's arm and pressed it.

"The smell of London. By God, it's grand."

He rejoiced in the noise and the bustle, and the crowd of people who jostled them; the radiance of the arc-lamps and the black shadows they cast, sharp but full-toned, gave him a sense of elation. They got out into the street and the porter went off to get them a taxi. Alban's eyes glittered as he looked at the buses and the policemen trying to direct the confusion. His distinguished face bore a look of something like inspiration. The taxi came. Their luggage was stowed away and piled up beside the driver, Alban gave the porter half-a-crown, and they drove off. They turned down Gracechurch Street and in Cannon Street were held up by a block in the traffic. Alban laughed out loud.

"What's the matter?" said Anne.

"I'm so excited."

They went along the Embankment. It was relatively quiet there. Taxis and cars passed them. The bells of the trams were music in his ears. At Westminster Bridge they cut across Parliament Square and drove through the green silence of St. James's Park. They had engaged a room at a hotel just off Jermyn Street. The reception clerk took them upstairs and a porter brought up their luggage. It was a room with twin beds and a bathroom.

"This looks all right," said Alban. "It'll do us till we can find a flat or something."

He looked at his watch.

"Look here, darling, we shall only fall over one another if we try to unpack together. We've got oodles of time and it'll take you longer to get straight and dress than me. I'll clear out. I want to go to the club and see if there's any mail for me. I've got my dinner jacket in my suit-case and it'll only take me twenty minutes to have a bath and dress. Does that suit you?"

"Yes. That's all right."

"I'll be back in an hour."

"Very well."

He took out of his pocket the little comb he always carried and passed it through his long fair hair. Then he put on his hat. He gave himself a glance in the mirror.

"Shall I turn on the bath for you?"

"No, don't bother."

"All right. So long."

He went out.

When he was gone Anne took her dressing-case and her hat-box and put them on the top of her trunk. Then she rang the bell. She did not take off her hat. She sat down and lit a cigarette. When a servant answered the bell she asked for the porter. He came. She pointed to the luggage.

"Will you take those things and leave them in the hall for the present. I'll tell you what to do with them presently."

"Very good, ma'am."

She gave him a florin. He took the trunk out and the other packages and closed the door behind him. A few tears slid down Anne's cheeks, but she shook herself; she dried her eyes and powdered her face. She needed all her calm. She was glad that Alban had conceived the idea of going to his club. It made things easier and gave her a little time to think them out.

Now that the moment had come to do what she had for weeks determined, now that she must say the terrible things she had to say, she quailed. Her heart sank. She knew exactly what she meant to say to Alban, she had made up her mind about that long ago, and had said the very words to herself a hundred times, three or four times a day every day of the long journey from Singapore, but she was afraid that she would grow confused. She dreaded an argument. The thought of a scene made her feel slightly sick. It was something at all events to have an hour in which to collect herself. He would say she was heartless and cruel and unreasonable. She could not help it.

"No, no, no," she cried aloud.

She shuddered with horror. And all at once she saw herself again in the bungalow, sitting as she had been sitting when the whole thing started. It was getting on towards tiffin time and in a few minutes Alban would be back from the office. It gave her pleasure to reflect that it was an attractive room for him to come back to, the large verandah which was their parlour, and she knew that though they had been there eighteen months he was still alive to the success she had made of it. The jalousies were drawn now against the midday sun and the mellowed light filtering through them gave an impression of cool silence. Anne was house-proud, and though they were moved from district to district according to the exigencies of the Service and seldom stayed anywhere very long, at each new post she started with new enthusiasm to make their house cosy and charming. She was very modern. Visitors were surprised because there were no knick-knacks. They were taken aback by the bold colour of her curtains and could not at all make out the tinted reproductions of pictures by Marie Laurencin and Gauguin in silvered frames which were placed on the walls with such cunning skill. She was conscious that few of them quite approved and the good ladies of Port Wallace and Pemberton thought such arrangements odd, affected and out of place; but this left her calm. They would learn. It did them good to get a bit of a jolt. And now she looked round the long, spacious verandah with the complacent sigh of the artist satisfied with his work. It was gay. It was bare. It was restful. It refreshed the spirit and gently excited the fancy. Three immense bowls of yellow cannas completed the colour scheme. Her eyes lingered for a moment on the book-shelves filled with books; that was another thing that disconcerted the colony, all the books they had, and strange books too, heavy they thought them for the most part; and she gave them a little affectionate look as though they were living things. Then she gave the piano a glance. A piece of music was still open on the rack, it was something of Debussy, and Alban had been playing it before he went to the office.

Her friends in the colony had condoled with her when Alban was appointed D.O. at Daktar, for it was the most isolated district in Sondurah. It was connected with the town which was the headquarters of the Government neither by telegraph nor telephone. But she liked it. They had been there for some time and she hoped they would remain till Alban went home on leave in another twelve months. It was as large as an English county, with a long coast-line, and the sea was dotted with little islands. A broad, winding river ran through it and on each side of this stretched hills densely covered with virgin forest. The station, a good way up the river, consisted of a row of Chinese shops and a native village nestling amid coconut trees, the District Office, the D.O.'s bungalow, the clerk's quarters and the barracks. Their only neighbours were the manager of a rubber estate a few miles up the river and the manager and his assistant, Dutchmen both, of a timber camp on one of the river's tributaries. The rubber estate's launch went up and down twice a month and was their only means of regular communication with the outside world. But though they were lonely they were not dull. Their days were full. Their ponies waited for them at dawn and they rode while the day was still fresh and in the bridle-paths through the jungle lingered the mystery of the tropical night. They came back, bathed, changed and had breakfast, and Alban went to the office. Anne spent the morning writing letters and working. She had fallen in love with the country from the first day she arrived in it and had taken pains to master the common language spoken. Her imagination was inflamed by the stories she heard of love and jealousy and death. She was told romantic tales of a time that was only just past. She sought to steep herself in the lore of those strange people. Both she and Alban read a great deal. They had for the country a considerable library and new books came from London by nearly every mail. Little that was noteworthy escaped them. Alban was fond of playing the piano. For an amateur he played very well. He had studied rather seriously, and he had an agreeable touch and a good ear; he could read music with ease, and it was always a pleasure to Anne to sit by him and follow the score when he tried something new. But their great delight was to tour the district. Sometimes they would be away for a fortnight at a time. They would go down the river in a prahu and then sail from one little island to another, bathe in the sea, and fish, or else row upstream till it grew shallow and the trees on either bank were so close to one another that you only saw a slim strip of sky between. Here the boatmen had to pole and they would spend the night in a native house. They bathed in a river pool so clear that you could see the sand shining silver at the bottom; and the spot was so lovely, so peaceful and remote, that you felt you could stay there for ever. Sometimes, on the other hand, they would tramp for days along the jungle paths, sleeping under canvas, and notwithstanding the mosquitoes that tormented them and the leeches that sucked their blood, enjoy every moment. Whoever slept so well as on a camp bed? And then there was the gladness of getting back, the delight in the comfort of the well-ordered establishment, the mail that had arrived with letters from home and all the papers, and the piano.

Alban would sit down to it then, his fingers itching to feel the keys, and in what he played, Stravinsky, Ravel, Darius Milhaud, she seemed to feel that he put in something of his own, the sounds of the jungle at night, dawn over the estuary, the starry nights and the crystal clearness of the forest pools.

Sometimes the rain fell in sheets for days at a time. Then Alban worked at Chinese. He was learning it so that he could communicate with the Chinese of the country in their own language, and Anne did the thousand-and-one things for which she had not had time before. Those days brought them even more closely together; they always had plenty to talk about, and when they were occupied with their separate affairs they were pleased to feel in their bones that they were near to one another. They were wonderfully united. The rainy days that shut them up within the walls of the bungalow made them feel as if they were one body in face of the world.

On occasion they went to Port Wallace. It was a change, but Anne was always glad to get home. She was never quite at her ease there. She was conscious that none of the people they met liked Alban. They were very ordinary people, middle-class and suburban and dull, without any of the intellectual interests that made life so full and varied to Alban and her, and many of them were narrow-minded and ill-natured; but since they had to pass the better part of their lives in contact with them, it was tiresome that they should feel so unkindly towards Alban. They said he was conceited. He was always very pleasant with them, but she was aware that they resented his cordiality. When he tried to be jovial they said he was putting on airs, and when he chaffed them they thought he was being funny at their expense.

Once they stayed at Government House, and Mrs. Hannay, the Governor's wife, who liked her, talked to her about it. Perhaps the Governor had suggested that she should give Anne a hint.

"You know, my dear, it's a pity your husband doesn't try to be more come-hither with people. He's very intelligent; don't you think it would be better if he didn't let others see he knows it quite so clearly? My husband said to me only yesterday: Of course I know Alban Torel is the cleverest young man in the Service, but he does manage to put my back up more than anyone I know. I am the Governor, but when he talks to me he always gives me the impression that he looks upon me as a damned fool."

The worst of it was that Anne knew how low an opinion Alban had of the Governor's parts.

"He doesn't mean to be superior," Anne answered, smiling. "And he really isn't in the least conceited. I think it's only because he has a straight nose and high cheek-bones."

"You know, they don't like him at the club. They call him Powder-Puff Percy."

Anne flushed. She had heard that before and it made her very angry. Her eyes filled with tears.

"I think it's frightfully unfair."

Mrs. Hannay took her hand and gave it an affectionate little squeeze.

"My dear, you know I don't want to hurt your feelings. Your husband can't help rising very high in the Service. He'd make things so much easier for himself if he were a little more human. Why doesn't he play football?"

"It's not his game. He's always only too glad to play tennis."

"He doesn't give that impression. He gives the impression that there's no one here who's worth his while to play with."

"Well, there isn't," said Anne, stung.

Alban happened to be an extremely good tennis-player. He had played a lot of tournaments in England and Anne knew that it gave him a grim satisfaction to knock those beefy, hearty men all over the court. He could make the best of them look foolish. He could be maddening on the tennis court and Anne was aware that sometimes he could not resist the temptation.

"He does play to the gallery, doesn't he?" said Mrs. Hannay.

"I don't think so. Believe me, Alban has no idea he isn't popular. As far as I can see he's always pleasant and friendly with everybody."

"It's then he's most offensive," said Mrs. Hannay dryly.

"I know people don't like us very much," said Anne, smiling a little. "I'm very sorry, but really I don't know what we can do about it."

"Not you, my dear," cried Mrs. Hannay. "Everybody adores you. That's why they put up with your husband. My dear, who could help liking you?"

"I don't know why they should adore me," said Anne.

But she did not say it quite sincerely. She was deliberately playing the part of the dear little woman and within her she bubbled with amusement. They disliked Alban because he had such an air of distinction, and because he was interested in art and literature; they did not understand these things and so thought them unmanly; and they disliked him because his capacity was greater than theirs. They disliked him because he was better bred than they. They thought him superior; well, he was superior, but not in the sense they meant. They forgave her because she was an ugly little thing. That was what she called herself, but she wasn't that, or if she was it was with an ugliness that was most attractive. She was like a little monkey, but a very sweet little monkey and very human. She had a neat figure. That was her best point. That and her eyes. They were very large, of a deep brown, liquid and shining; they were full of fun, but they could be tender on occasion with a charming sympathy. She was dark, her frizzy hair was almost black, and her skin was swarthy; she had a small fleshy nose, with large nostrils, and much too big a mouth. But she was alert and vivacious. She could talk with a show of real interest to the ladies of the colony about their husbands and their servants and their children in England, and she could listen appreciatively to the men who told her stories that she had often heard before. They thought her a jolly good sort. They did not know what clever fun she made of them in private. It never occurred to them that she thought them narrow, gross and pretentious. They found no glamour in the East because they looked at it vulgarly with material eyes. Romance lingered at their threshold and they drove it away like an importunate beggar. She was aloof. She repeated to herself Landor's line:

"Nature I loved, and next to nature, art."

She reflected on her conversation with Mrs. Hannay, but on the whole it left her unconcerned. She wondered whether she should say anything about it to Alban; it had always seemed a little odd to her that he should be so little aware of his unpopularity; but she was afraid that if she told him of it he would become self-conscious. He never noticed the coldness of the men at the club. He made them feel shy and therefore uncomfortable. His appearance then caused a sort of awkwardness, but he, happily insensible, was breezily cordial to all and sundry. The fact was that he was strangely unconscious of other people. She was in a class by herself, she and a little group of friends they had in London, but he could never quite realise that the people of the colony, the government officials and the planters and their wives, were human beings. They were to him like pawns in a game. He laughed with them, chaffed them, and was amiably tolerant of them; with a chuckle Anne told herself that he was rather like the master of a preparatory school taking little boys out on a picnic and anxious to give them a good time.

She was afraid it wasn't much good telling Alban. He was incapable of the dissimulation which, she happily realised, came so easily to her. What was one to do with these people? The men had come out to the colony as lads from second-rate schools, and life had taught them nothing. At fifty they had the outlook of hobbledehoys. Most of them drank a great deal too much. They read nothing worth reading. Their ambition was to be like everybody else. Their highest praise was to say that a man was a damned good sort. If you were interested in the things of the spirit you were a prig. They were eaten up with envy of one another and devoured by petty jealousies. And the women, poor things, were obsessed by petty rivalries. They made a circle that was more provincial than any in the smallest town in England. They were prudish and spiteful. What did it matter if they did not like Alban? They would have to put up with him because his ability was so great. He was clever and energetic. They could not say that he did not do his work well. He had been successful in every post he had occupied. With his sensitiveness and his imagination he understood the native mind and he was able to get the natives to do things that no one in his position could. He had a gift for languages, and he spoke all the local dialects. He not only knew the common tongue that most of the government officials spoke, but was acquainted with the niceties of the language and on occasion could make use of a ceremonial speech that flattered and impressed the chiefs. He had a gift for organisation. He was not afraid of responsibility. In due course he was bound to be made a Resident. Alban had some interest in England; his father was a brigadier-general killed in the war, and though he had no private means he had influential friends. He spoke of them with pleasant irony.

"The great advantage of democratic government," he said, "is that merit, with influence to back it, can be pretty sure of receiving its due reward."

Alban was so obviously the ablest man in the Service that there seemed no reason why he should not eventually be made Governor. Then, thought Anne, his air of superiority, of which they complained, would be in place. They would accept him as their master and he would know how to make himself respected and obeyed. The position she foresaw did not dazzle her. She accepted it as a right. It would be fun for Alban to be Governor and for her to be the Governor's wife. And what an opportunity! They were sheep, the government servants and the planters; when Government House was the seat of culture they would soon fall into line. When the best way to the Governor's favour was to be intelligent, intelligence would become the fashion. She and Alban would cherish the native arts and collect carefully the memorials of a vanished past. The country would make an advance it had never dreamed of. They would develop it, but along lines of order and beauty. They would instil into their subordinates a passion for that beautiful land and a loving interest in these romantic races. They would make them realise what music meant. They would cultivate literature. They would create beauty. It would be the golden age.

Suddenly she heard Alban's footstep. Anne awoke from her day-dream. All that was far away in the future. Alban was only a District Officer yet and what was important was the life they were living now. She heard Alban go into the bath-house and splash water over himself. In a minute he came in. He had changed into a shirt and shorts. His fair hair was still wet.

"Tiffin ready?" he asked.

"Yes."

He sat down at the piano and played the piece that he had played in the morning. The silvery notes cascaded coolly down the sultry air. You had an impression of a formal garden with great trees and elegant pieces of artificial water and of leisurely walks bordered with pseudo-classical statues. Alban played with a peculiar delicacy. Lunch was announced by the head boy. He rose from the piano. They walked into the dining-room hand in hand. A punkah lazily fanned the air. Anne gave the table a glance. With its bright-coloured tablecloth and the amusing plates it looked very gay.

"Anything exciting at the office this morning?" she asked.

"No, nothing much. A buffalo case. Oh, and Prynne has sent along to ask me to go up to the estate. Some coolies have been damaging the trees and he wants me to come along and look into it."

Prynne was manager of the rubber estate up the river and now and then they spent a night with him. Sometimes when he wanted a change he came down to dinner and slept at the D.O.'s bungalow. They both liked him. He was a man of five-and-thirty, with a red face, with deep furrows in it, and very black hair. He was quite uneducated, but cheerful and easy, and being the only Englishman within two days' journey they could not but be friendly with him. He had been a little shy of them at first. News spreads quickly in the East and long before they arrived in the district he heard that they were highbrows. He did not know what he would make of them. He probably did not know that he had charm, which makes up for many more commendable qualities, and Alban with his almost feminine sensibilities was peculiarly susceptible to this. He found Alban much more human than he expected, and of course Anne was stunning. Alban played ragtime for him, which he would not have done for the Governor, and played dominoes with him. When Alban was making his first tour of the district with Anne, and suggested that they would like to spend a couple of nights on the estate, he had thought it as well to warn him that he lived with a native woman and had two children by her. He would do his best to keep them out of Anne's sight, but he could not send them away, there was nowhere to send them. Alban laughed.

"Anne isn't that sort of woman at all. Don't dream of hiding them. She loves children."

Anne quickly made friends with the shy, pretty little native woman and soon was playing happily with the children. She and the girl had long confidential chats. The children took a fancy to her. She brought them lovely toys from Port Wallace. Prynne, comparing her smiling tolerance with the disapproving acidity of the other white women of the colony, described himself as knocked all of a heap. He could not do enough to show his delight and gratitude.

"If all highbrows are like you," he said, "give me highbrows every time."

He hated to think that in another year they would leave the district for good and the chances were that, if the next D.O. was married, his wife would think it dreadful that, rather than live alone, he had a native woman to live with him and, what was more, was much attached to her.

But there had been a good deal of discontent on the estate of late. The coolies were Chinese and infected with communist ideas. They were disorderly. Alban had been obliged to sentence several of them for various crimes to terms of imprisonment.

"Prynne tells me that as soon as their term is up he's going to send them all back to China and get Javanese instead," said Alban. "I'm sure he's right. They're much more amenable."

"You don't think there's going to be any serious trouble?"

"Oh, no. Prynne knows his job and he's a pretty determined fellow. He wouldn't put up with any nonsense and with me and our policemen to back him up I don't imagine they'll try any monkey tricks." He smiled. "The iron hand in the velvet glove."

The words were barely out of his mouth when a sudden shouting arose. There was a commotion and the sound of steps. Loud voices and cries.

"Tuan, Tuan."

"What the devil's the matter?"

Alban sprang from his chair and went swiftly on to

the verandah. Anne followed him. At the bottom of the steps was a group of natives. There was the sergeant, and three or four policemen, boatmen and several men from the kampong.

"What is it?" called Alban.

Two or three shouted back in answer. The sergeant pushed others aside and Alban saw lying on the ground a man in a shirt and khaki shorts. He ran down the steps. He recognised the man as the assistant manager of Prynne's estate. He was a half-caste. His shorts were covered with blood and there was clotted blood all over one side of his face and head. He was unconscious.

"Bring him up here," called Anne.

Alban gave an order. The man was lifted up and carried on to the verandah. They laid him on the floor and Anne put a pillow under his head. She sent for water and for the medicine-chest in which they kept things for emergency.

"Is he dead?" asked Alban.

"No."

"Better try to give him some brandy."

The boatmen brought ghastly news. The Chinese coolies had risen suddenly and attacked the manager's office. Prynne was killed and the assistant manager, Oakley by name, had escaped only by the skin of his teeth. He had come upon the rioters when they were looting the office, he had seen Prynne's body thrown out of the window, and had taken to his heels. Some of the Chinese saw him and gave chase. He ran for the river and was wounded as he jumped into the launch. The launch managed to put off before the Chinese could get on board and they had come down-stream for help as fast as they could go. As they went they saw flames rising from the office buildings. There was no doubt that the coolies had burned down everything that would burn.

Oakley gave a groan and opened his eyes. He was a

little, darkskinned man, with flattened features and thick coarse hair. His great native eyes were filled with terror.

"You're all right," said Anne. "You're quite safe."

He gave a sigh and smiled. Anne washed his face and swabbed it with antiseptics. The wound on his head was not serious.

"Can you speak yet?" said Alban.

"Wait a bit," she said. "We must look at his leg."

Alban ordered the sergeant to get the crowd out of the verandah. Anne ripped up one leg of the shorts. The material was clinging to the coagulated wound.

"I've been bleeding like a pig," said Oakley.

It was only a flesh wound. Alban was clever with his fingers, and though the blood began to flow again they stanched it. Alban put on a dressing and a bandage. The sergeant and a policeman lifted Oakley on to a long chair. Alban gave him a brandy and soda, and soon he felt strong enough to speak. He knew no more than the boatmen had already told. Prynne was dead and the estate was in flames.

"And the girl and the children?" asked Anne.

"I don't know."

"Oh, Alban."

"I must turn out the police. Are you sure Prynne is dead?"

"Yes, sir. I saw him."

"Have the rioters got fire-arms?"

"I don't know, sir."

"How d'you mean, you don't know?" Alban cried irritably. "Prynne had a gun, hadn't he?"

"Yes, sir."

"There must have been more on the estate. You had one, didn't you? The head overseer had one."

The half-caste was silent. Alban looked at him sternly.

"How many of those damned Chinese are there?"

"A hundred and fifty."

Anne wondered that he asked so many questions. It

seemed waste of time. The important thing was to collect coolies for the transport up-river, prepare the boats and issue ammunition to the police.

"How many policemen have you got, sir?" asked Oakley.

"Eight and the sergeant."

"Could I come too? That would make ten of us. I'm sure I shall be all right now I'm bandaged."

"I'm not going," said Alban.

"Alban, you must," cried Anne. She could not believe her ears.

"Nonsense. It would be madness. Oakley's obviously useless. He's sure to have a temperature in a few hours. He'd only be in the way. That leaves nine guns. There are a hundred and fifty Chinese and they've got fire-arms and all the ammunition in the world."

"How d'you know?"

"It stands to reason they wouldn't have started a show like this unless they had. It would be idiotic to go."

Anne stared at him with open mouth. Oakley's eyes were puzzled.

"What are you going to do?"

"Well, fortunately we've got the launch. I'll send it to Port Wallace with a request for reinforcements."

"But they won't be here for two days at least."

"Well, what of it? Prynne's dead and the estate burned to the ground. We couldn't do any good by going up now. I shall send a native to reconnoitre so that we can find out exactly what the rioters are doing." He gave Anne his charming smile. "Believe me, my pet, the rascals won't lose anything by waiting a day or two for what's coming to them."

Oakley opened his mouth to speak, but perhaps he hadn't the nerve. He was a half-caste assistant manager and Alban, the D.O., represented the power of the Government. But the man's eyes sought Anne's and she thought she read in them an earnest and personal appeal.

"But in two days they're capable of committing the most frightful atrocities," she cried. "It's quite unspeakable what they may do."

"Whatever damage they do they'll pay for. I promise you that."

"Oh, Alban, you can't sit still and do nothing. I beseech you to go yourself at once."

"Don't be so silly. I can't quell a riot with eight policemen and a sergeant. I haven't got the right to take a risk of that sort. We'd have to go in boats. You don't think we could get up unobserved. The lalang along the banks is perfect cover and they could just take pot shots at us as we came along. We shouldn't have a chance."

"I'm afraid they'll only think it weakness if nothing is done for two days, sir," said Oakley.

"When I want your opinion I'll ask for it," said Alban acidly. "So far as I can see when there was danger the only thing you did was to cut and run. I can't persuade myself that your assistance in a crisis would be very valuable."

The half-caste reddened. He said nothing more. He looked straight in front of him with troubled eyes.

"I'm going down to the office," said Alban. "I'll just write a short report and send it down the river by launch at once."

He gave an order to the sergeant, who had been standing all this time stiffly at the top of the steps. He saluted and ran off. Alban went into a little hall they had to get his topee. Anne swiftly followed him.

"Alban, for God's sake listen to me a minute," she whispered.

"I don't want to be rude to you, darling, but I am pressed for time. I think you'd much better mind your own business."

"You can't do nothing, Alban. You must go. Whatever the risk."

"Don't be such a fool," he said angrily.

He had never been angry with her before. She seized his hand to hold him back.

"I tell you I can do no good by going."

"You don't know. There's the woman and Prynne's children. We must do something to save them. Let me come with you. They'll kill them."

"They've probably killed them already."

"Oh, how can you be so callous! If there's a chance of saving them it's your duty to try."

"It's my duty to act like a reasonable human being. I'm not going to risk my life and my policemen's for the sake of a native woman and her half-caste brats. What sort of a damned fool do you take me for?"

"They'll say you were afraid."

"Who?"

"Everyone in the colony."

He smiled disdainfully.

"If you only knew what a complete contempt I have for the opinion of everyone in the colony."

She gave him a long searching look. She had been married to him for eight years and she knew every expression of his face and every thought in his mind. She stared into his blue eyes as if they were open windows. She suddenly went quite pale. She dropped his hand and turned away. Without another word she went back on to the verandah. Her ugly little monkey face was a mask of horror.

Alban went to his office, wrote a brief account of the facts, and in a few minutes the motor launch was pounding down the river.

The next two days were endless. Escaped natives brought them news of happenings on the estate. But from their excited and terrified stories it was impossible to get an exact impression of the truth. There had been a good deal of bloodshed. The head overseer had been killed. They brought wild tales of cruelty and outrage.

Anne could hear nothing of Prynne's woman and the two children. She shuddered when she thought of what might have been their fate. Alban collected as many natives as he could. They were armed with spears and swords. He commandeered boats. The situation was serious, but he kept his head. He felt that he had done all that was possible and nothing remained but for him to carry on normally. He did his official work. He played the piano a great deal. He rode with Anne in the early morning. He appeared to have forgotten that they had had the first serious difference of opinion in the whole of their married life. He took it that Anne had accepted the wisdom of his decision. He was as amusing, cordial and gay with her as he had always been. When he spoke of the rioters it was with grim irony: when the time came to settle matters a good many of them would wish they had never been born.

"What'll happen to them?" asked Anne.

"Oh, they'll hang." He gave a shrug of distaste. "I hate having to be present at executions. It always makes me feel rather sick."

He was very sympathetic to Oakley, whom they had put to bed and whom Anne was nursing. Perhaps he was sorry that in the exasperation of the moment he had spoken to him offensively, and he went out of his way to be nice to him.

Then on the afternoon of the third day, when they were drinking their coffee after luncheon, Alban's quick ears caught the sound of a motor boat approaching. At the same moment a policeman ran up to say that the government launch was sighted.

"At last," cried Alban.

He bolted out of the house. Anne raised one of the jalousies and looked out at the river. Now the sound was quite loud and in a moment she saw the boat come round the bend. She saw Alban on the landing-stage. He got into a prahu and as the launch dropped her anchor he went on board. She told Oakley that the reinforcements had come.

"Will the D.O. go up with them when they attack?" he asked her.

"Naturally," said Anne coldly.

"I wondered."

Anne felt a strange feeling in her heart. For the last two days she had had to exercise all her self-control not to cry. She did not answer. She went out of the room.

A quarter of an hour later Alban returned to the bungalow with the captain of constabulary who had been sent with twenty Sikhs to deal with the rioters. Captain Stratton was a little red-faced man with a red moustache and bow legs, very hearty and dashing, whom she had met often at Port Wallace.

"Well, Mrs. Torel, this is a pretty kettle of fish," he cried, as he shook hands with her, in a loud jolly voice. "Here I am, with my army all full of pep and ready for a scrap. Up, boys, and at 'em. Have you got anything to drink in this benighted place?"

"Boy," she cried, smiling.

"Something long and cool and faintly alcoholic, and then I'm ready to discuss the plan of campaign."

His breeziness was very comforting. It blew away the sullen apprehension that had seemed ever since the disaster to brood over the lost peace of the bungalow. The boy came in with a tray and Stratton mixed himself a stengah. Alban put him in possession of the facts. He told them clearly, briefly and with precision.

"I must say I admire you," said Stratton. "In your place I should never have been able to resist the temptation to take my eight cops and have a whack at the blighters myself."

"I thought it was a perfectly unjustifiable risk to take."

"Safety first, old boy, eh, what?" said Stratton jovially. "I'm jolly glad you didn't. It's not often we get the chance of a scrap. It would have been a dirty trick to keep the whole show to yourself."

Captain Stratton was all for steaming straight up the river and attacking at once, but Alban pointed out to him the inadvisability of such a course. The sound of the approaching launch would warn the rioters. The long grass at the river's edge offered them cover and they had enough guns to make a landing difficult. It seemed useless to expose the attacking force to their fire. It was silly to forget that they had to face a hundred and fifty desperate men and it would be easy to fall into an ambush. Alban expounded his own plan. Stratton listened to it. He nodded now and then. The plan was evidently a good one. It would enable them to take the rioters on the rear, surprise them, and in all probability finish the job without a single casualty. He would have been a fool not to accept it.

"But why didn't you do that yourself?" asked Stratton.

"With eight men and a sergeant?"

Stratton did not answer.

"Anyhow it's not a bad idea and we'll settle on it. It gives us plenty of time, so with your permission, Mrs. Torel, I'll have a bath."

They set out at sunset, Captain Stratton and his twenty Sikhs, Alban with his policemen and the natives he had collected. The night was dark and moonless. Trailing behind them were the dug-outs that Alban had gathered together and into which after a certain distance they proposed to transfer their force. It was important that no sound should give warning of their approach. After they had gone for about three hours by launch they took to the dug-outs and in them silently paddled up-stream. They reached the border of the vast estate and landed. Guides led them along a path so narrow that they had to march in single file. It had been long unused and the going was heavy. They had twice to ford a stream. The path led them circuitously to the rear of the coolie lines, but they did not wish to reach them till nearly dawn and presently Stratton gave the order to halt. It was a long cold wait. At last the night seemed to be less dark; you did not see the trunks of the trees, but were vaguely sensible of them against its darkness. Stratton had been sitting with his back to a tree. He gave a whispered order to a sergeant and in a few minutes the column was once more on the march. Suddenly they found themselves on a road. They formed fours. The dawn broke and in the ghostly light the surrounding objects were wanly visible. The column stopped on a whispered order. They had come in sight of the coolie lines. Silence reigned in them. The column crept on again and again halted. Stratton, his eyes shining, gave Alban a smile.

"We've caught the blighters asleep."

He lined up his men. They inserted cartridges in their guns. He stepped forward and raised his hand. The carbines were pointed at the coolie lines.

"Fire."

There was a rattle as the volley of shots rang out. Then suddenly there was a tremendous din and the Chinese poured out, shouting and waving their arms, but in front of them, to Alban's utter bewilderment, bellowing at the top of his voice and shaking his fist at them, was a white man.

"Who the hell's that?" cried Stratton.

A very big, very fat man, in khaki trousers and a singlet, was running towards them as fast as his fat legs would carry him and as he ran shaking both fists at them and yelling:

"Smerige flikkers! Verlockte ploerten!"

"My God, it's Van Hasseldt," said Alban.

This was the Dutch manager of the timber camp which was situated on a considerable tributary of the river about twenty miles away.

"What the hell do you think you're doing?" he puffed as he came up to them.

"How the hell did you get here?" asked Stratton in turn.

He saw that the Chinese were scattering in all directions and gave his men instructions to round them up. Then he turned again to Van Hasseldt.

"What's it mean?"

"Mean? Mean?" shouted the Dutchman furiously. "That's what I want to know. You and your damned policemen. What do you mean by coming here at this hour in the morning and firing a damned volley. Target practice? You might have killed me. Idiots!"

"Have a cigarette," said Stratton.

"How did you get here, Van Hasseldt?" asked Alban again, very much at sea. "This is the force they've sent from Port Wallace to quell the riot."

"How did I get here? I walked. How did you think I got here? Riot be damned. I quelled the riot. If that's what you came for you can take your damned policemen home again. A bullet came within a foot of my head."

"I don't understand," said Alban.

"There's nothing to understand," spluttered Van Hasseldt, still fuming. "Some coolies came to my estate and said the Chinks had killed Prynne and burned the bally place down, so I took my assistant and my head overseer and a Dutch friend I had staying with me and came over to see what the trouble was."

Captain Stratton opened his eyes wide.

"Did you just stroll in as if it was a picnic?" he asked.

"Well, you don't think after all the years I've been in this country I'm going to let a couple of hundred Chinks put the fear of God into me? I found them all scared out of their lives. One of them had the nerve to pull a gun on me and I blew his bloody brains out. And the rest surrendered. I've got the leaders tied up. I was going to send a boat down to you this morning to come up and get them."

Stratton stared at him for a minute and then burst into

a shout of laughter. He laughed till the tears ran down his face. The Dutchman looked at him angrily, then began to laugh too; he laughed with the big belly laugh of a very fat man and his coils of fat heaved and shook. Alban watched them sullenly. He was very angry.

"What about Prynne's girl and the kids?" he asked.

"Oh, they got away all right."

It just showed how wise he had been not to let himself be influenced by Anne's hysteria. Of course the children had come to no harm. He never thought they would.

Van Hasseldt and his little party started back for the timber camp, and as soon after as possible Stratton embarked his twenty Sikhs and leaving Alban with his sergeant and his policemen to deal with the situation departed for Port Wallace. Alban gave him a brief report for the Governor. There was much for him to do. It looked as though he would have to stay for a considerable time; but since every house on the estate had been burned to the ground and he was obliged to instal himself in the coolie lines he thought it better that Anne should not join him. He sent her a note to that effect. He was glad to be able to reassure her of the safety of poor Prynne's girl. He set to work at once to make his preliminary enquiry. He examined a host of witnesses. But a week later he received an order to go to Port Wallace at once. The launch that brought it was to take him and he was able to see Anne on the way down for no more than an hour. Alban was a trifle vexed.

"I don't know why the Governor can't leave me to get things straight without dragging me off like this. It's extremely inconvenient."

"Oh, well, the Government never bothers very much about the convenience of its subordinates, does it?" smiled Anne.

"It's just red-tape. I would offer to take you along, darling, only I shan't stay a minute longer than I need. I want to get my evidence together for the Sessions Court as soon as possible. I think in a country like this it's very important that justice should be prompt."

When the launch came in to Port Wallace one of the harbour police told him that the harbour-master had a chit for him. It was from the Governor's secretary and informed him that His Excellency desired to see him as soon as convenient after his arrival. It was ten in the morning. Alban went to the club, had a bath and shaved, and then in clean ducks, his hair neatly brushed, he called a rickshaw and told the boy to take him to the Governor's office. He was at once shown in to the secretary's room. The secretary shook hands with him.

"I'll tell H.E. you're here," he said. "Won't you sit down?"

The secretary left the room and in a little while came back.

"H.E. will see you in a minute. Do you mind if I get on with my letters?"

Alban smiled. The secretary was not exactly come-hither. He waited, smoking a cigarette, and amused himself with his own thoughts. He was making a good job of the preliminary enquiry. It interested him. Then an orderly came in and told Alban that the Governor was ready for him. He rose from his seat and followed him into the Governor's room.

"Good-morning, Torel."

"Good-morning, sir."

The Governor was sitting at a large desk. He nodded to Alban and motioned to him to take a seat. The Governor was all grey. His hair was grey, his face, his eyes; he looked as though the tropical suns had washed the colour out of him; he had been in the country for thirty years and had risen one by one through all the ranks of the Service; he looked tired and depressed. Even his voice was grey. Alban liked him because he was quiet; he did not think him clever, but he had an unrivalled knowledge of the country, and his great experience was a very good substitute for intelligence. He looked at Alban for a full moment without speaking and the odd idea came to Alban that he was embarrassed. He very nearly gave him a lead.

"I saw Van Hasseldt yesterday," said the Governor suddenly.

"Yes, sir?"

"Will you give me your account of the occurrences at the Alud Estate and of the steps you took to deal with them."

Alban had an orderly mind. He was self-possessed. He marshalled his facts well and was able to state them with precision. He chose his words with care and spoke them fluently.

"You had a sergeant and eight policemen. Why did you not immediately go to the scene of the disturbance?"

"I thought the risk was unjustifiable."

A thin smile was outlined on the Governor's grey face.

"If the officers of this Government had hesitated to take unjustifiable risks it would never have become a province of the British Empire."

Alban was silent. It was difficult to talk to a man who spoke obvious nonsense.

"I am anxious to hear your reasons for the decision you took."

Alban gave them coolly. He was quite convinced of the rightness of his action. He repeated, but more fully, what he had said in the first place to Anne. The Governor listened attentively.

"Van Hasseldt, with his manager, a Dutch friend of his, and a native overseer, seems to have coped with the situation very efficiently," said the Governor.

"He had a lucky break. That doesn't prevent him from being a damned fool. It was madness to do what he did."

"Do you realise that by leaving a Dutch planter to do what you should have done yourself, you have covered the Government with ridicule?"

"No, sir."

"You've made yourself a laughing-stock in the whole colony."

Alban smiled.

"My back is broad enough to bear the ridicule of persons to whose opinion I am entirely indifferent."

"The utility of a government official depends very largely on his prestige, and I'm afraid his prestige is likely to be inconsiderable when he lies under the stigma of cowardice."

Alban flushed a little.

"I don't quite know what you mean by that, sir."

"I've gone into the matter very carefully. I've seen Captain Stratton, and Oakley, poor Prynne's assistant, and I've seen Van Hasseldt. I've listened to your defence."

"I didn't know that I was defending myself, sir."

"Be so good as not to interrupt me. I think you committed a grave error of judgment. As it turns out, the risk was very small, but whatever it was, I think you should have taken it. In such matters promptness and firmness are essential. It is not for me to conjecture what motive led you to send for a force of constabulary and do nothing till they came. I am afraid, however, that I consider that your usefulness in the Service is no longer very great."

Alban looked at him with astonishment.

"But would you have gone under the circumstances?" he asked him.

"I should."

Alban shrugged his shoulders.

"Don't you believe me?" rapped out the Governor.

"Of course I believe you, sir. But perhaps you will allow me to say that if you had been killed the colony would have suffered an irreparable loss."

The Governor drummed on the table with his fingers. He looked out of the window and then looked again at

Alban. When he spoke it was not unkindly.

"I think you are unfitted by temperament for this rather rough-and-tumble life, Torel. If you'll take my advice you'll go home. With your abilities I feel sure that you'll soon find an occupation much better suited to you."

"I'm afraid I don't understand what you mean, sir."

"Oh, come, Torel, you're not stupid. I'm trying to make things easy for you. For your wife's sake as well as for your own I do not wish you to leave the colony with the stigma of being dismissed from the Service for cowardice. I'm giving you the opportunity of resigning."

"Thank you very much, sir. I'm not prepared to avail myself of the opportunity. If I resign I admit that I committed an error and that the charge you make against me is justified. I don't admit it."

"You can please yourself. I have considered the matter very carefully and I have no doubt about it in my mind. I am forced to discharge you from the Service. The necessary papers will reach you in due course. Meanwhile you will return to your post and hand over to the officer appointed to succeed you on his arrival."

"Very good, sir," replied Alban, a twinkle of amusement in his eyes. "When do you desire me to return to my post?"

"At once."

"Have you any objection to my going to the club and having tiffin before I go?"

The Governor looked at him with surprise. His exasperation was mingled with an unwilling admiration.

"Not at all. I'm sorry, Torel, that this unhappy incident should have deprived the Government of a servant whose zeal has always been so apparent and whose tact, intelligence and industry seemed to point him out in the future for very high office."

"Your Excellency does not read Schiller, I suppose.

You are probably not acquainted with his celebrated line: *mit der Dummheit kämpfen die Götter selbst vergebens.*"

"What does it mean?"

"Roughly: Against stupidity the gods themselves battle in vain."

"Good-morning."

With his head in the air, a smile on his lips, Alban left the Governor's office. The Governor was human, and he had the curiosity to ask his secretary later in the day if Alban Torel had really gone to the club.

"Yes, sir. He had tiffin there."

"It must have wanted some nerve."

Alban entered the club jauntily and joined the group of men standing at the bar. He talked to them in the breezy, cordial tone he always used with them. It was designed to put them at their ease. They had been discussing him ever since Stratton had come back to Port Wallace with his story, sneering at him and laughing at him, and all who had resented his superciliousness, and they were the majority, were triumphant because his pride had had a fall. But they were so taken aback at seeing him now, so confused to find him as confident as ever, that it was they who were embarrassed.

One man, though he knew perfectly, asked him what he was doing in Port Wallace.

"Oh, I came about the riot on the Alud Estate. H.E. wanted to see me. He does not see eye to eye with me about it. The silly old ass has fired me. I'm going home as soon as he appoints a D.O. to take over."

There was a moment of awkwardness. One, more kindly disposed than the others, said:

"I'm awfully sorry."

Alban shrugged his shoulders.

"My dear fellow, what can you do with a perfect damned fool? The only thing is to let him stew in his own juice."

When the Governor's secretary had told his chief as

much of this as he thought discreet, the Governor smiled.

"Courage is a queer thing. I would rather have shot myself than go to the club just then and face all those fellows."

A fortnight later, having sold to the incoming D.O. all the decorations that Anne had taken so much trouble about, with the rest of their things in packing-cases and trunks, they arrived at Port Wallace to await the local steamer that was to take them to Singapore. The padre's wife invited them to stay with her, but Anne refused; she insisted that they should go to the hotel. An hour after their arrival she received a very kind little letter from the Governor's wife asking her to go and have tea with her. She went. She found Mrs. Hannay alone, but in a minute the Governor joined them. He expressed his regret that she was leaving and told her how sorry he was for the cause.

"It's very kind of you to say that," said Anne, smiling gaily, "but you mustn't think I take it to heart. I'm entirely on Alban's side. I think what he did was absolutely right and if you don't mind my saying so I think you've treated him most unjustly."

"Believe me, I hated having to take the step I took."

"Don't let's talk about it," said Anne.

"What are your plans when you get home?" asked Mrs. Hannay.

Anne began to chat brightly. You would have thought she had not a care in the world. She seemed in great spirits at going home. She was jolly and amusing and made little jokes. When she took leave of the Governor and his wife she thanked them for all their kindness. The Governor escorted her to the door.

The next day but one, after dinner, they went on board the clean and comfortable little ship. The padre and his wife saw them off. When they went into their cabin they found a large parcel on Anne's bunk. It was addressed to Alban. He opened it and saw that it was an immense powder-puff.

"Hullo, I wonder who sent us this," he said, with a laugh. "It must be for you, darling."

Anne gave him a quick look. She went pale. The brutes! How could they be so cruel? She forced herself to smile.

"It's enormous, isn't it? I've never seen such a large powderpuff in my life."

But when he had left the cabin and they were out at sea, she threw it passionately overboard.

And now, now that they were back in London and Sondurah was nine thousand miles away, she clenched her hands as she thought of it. Somehow, it seemed the worst thing of all. It was so wantonly unkind to send that absurd object to Alban, Powder-Puff Percy; it showed such a petty spite. Was that their idea of humour? Nothing had hurt her more and even now she felt that it was only by holding on to herself that she could prevent herself from crying. Suddenly she started, for the door opened and Alban came in. She was still sitting in the chair in which he had left her.

"Hullo, why haven't you dressed?" He looked about the room. "You haven't unpacked."

"No."

"Why on earth not?"

"I'm not going to unpack. I'm not going to stay here. I'm leaving you."

"What are you talking about?"

"I've stuck it out till now. I made up my mind I would till we got home. I set my teeth, I've borne more than I thought it possible to bear, but now it's finished. I've done all that could be expected of me. We're back in London now and I can go."

He looked at her in utter bewilderment.

"Are you mad, Anne?"

"Oh, my God, what I've endured! The journey to

Singapore, with all the officers knowing, and even the Chinese stewards. And at Singapore, the way people looked at us at the hotel, and the sympathy I had to put up with, the bricks they dropped and their embarrassment when they realised what they'd done. My God, I could have killed them. That interminable journey home. There wasn't a single passenger on the ship who didn't know. The contempt they had for you and the kindness they went out of their way to show me. And you so self-complacent and so pleased with yourself, seeing nothing, feeling nothing. You must have the hide of a rhinoceros. The misery of seeing you so chatty and agreeable. Pariahs, that's what we were. You seemed to ask them to snub you. How can anyone be so shameless?"

She was flaming with passion. Now that at last she need not wear the mask of indifference and pride that she had forced herself to assume she cast aside all reserve and all self-control. The words poured from her trembling lips in a virulent stream.

"My dear, how can you be so absurd?" he said good-naturedly, smiling. "You must be very nervous and high-strung to have got such ideas in your head. Why didn't you tell me? You're like a country bumpkin who comes to London and thinks everyone is staring at him. Nobody bothered about us, and if they did what on earth did it matter? You ought to have more sense then to bother about what a lot of fools say. And what do you imagine they were saying?"

"They were saying you'd been fired."

"Well, that was true," he laughed.

"They said you were a coward."

"What of it?"

"Well, you see, that was true too."

He looked at her for a moment reflectively. His lips tightened a little.

"And what makes you think so?" he asked acidly.

"I saw it in your eyes, that day the news came, when you refused to go to the estate and I followed you into the hall when you went to fetch your topee. I begged you to go, I felt that whatever the danger you must take it, and suddenly I saw the fear in your eyes. I nearly fainted with the horror."

"I should have been a fool to risk my life to no purpose. Why should I? Nothing that concerned me was at stake. Courage is the obvious virtue of the stupid. I don't attach any particular importance to it."

"How do you mean that nothing that concerned you was at stake? If that's true then your whole life is a sham. You've given away everything you stood for, everything we both stand for. You've let all of us down. We did set ourselves up on a pinnacle, we did think ourselves better than the rest of them because we loved literature and art and music, we weren't content to live a life of ignoble jealousies and vulgar tittle-tattle, we did cherish the things of the spirit, and we loved beauty. It was our food and drink. They laughed at us and sneered at us. That was inevitable. The ignorant and the common naturally hate and fear those who are interested in things they don't understand. We didn't care. We called them Philistines. We despised them and we had a right to despise them. Our justification was that we were better and nobler and wiser and braver than they were. And you weren't better, you weren't nobler, you weren't braver. When the crisis came you slunk away like a whipped cur with his tail between his legs. You of all people hadn't the right to be a coward. They despise *us* now and they have the right to despise us. Us and all we stood for. Now they can say that art and beauty are all rot; when it comes to a pinch people like us always let you down. They never stopped looking for a chance to turn and rend us and you gave it to them. They can say that they always expected it. It's a triumph for them. I used to be furious because they called you Powder-Puff

Percy. Did you know they did?"

"Of course. I thought it very vulgar, but it left me entirely indifferent."

"It's funny that their instinct should have been so right."

"Do you mean to say you've been harbouring this against me all these weeks? I should never have thought you capable of it."

"I couldn't let you down when everyone was against you. I was too proud for that. Whatever happened I swore to myself that I'd stick to you till we got home. It's been torture."

"Don't you love me any more?"

"Love you? I loathe the very sight of you."

"Anne!"

"God knows I loved you. For eight years I worshipped the ground you trod on. You were everything to me. I believed in you as some people believe in God. When I saw the fear in your eyes that day, when you told me that you weren't going to risk your life for a kept woman and her half-caste brats, I was shattered. It was as though someone had wrenched my heart out of my body and trampled on it. You killed my love there and then, Alban. You killed it stone-dead. Since then when you've kissed me I've had to clench my hands so as not to turn my face away. The mere thought of anything else makes me feel physically sick. I loathe your complacence and your frightful insensitiveness. Perhaps I could have forgiven it if it had been just a moment's weakness and if afterwards you'd been ashamed. I should have been miserable, but I think my love was so great that I should only have felt pity for you. But you're incapable of shame. And now I believe in nothing. You're only a silly, pretentious vulgar poseur. I would rather be the wife of a second-rate planter so long as he had the common human virtues of a man than the wife of a fake like you."

He did not answer. Gradually his face began to

discompose. Those handsome, regular features of his horribly distorted and suddenly he broke out into loud sobs. She gave a little cry.

"Don't, Alban, don't."

"Oh, darling, how can you be so cruel to me? I adore you. I'd give my whole life to please you. I can't live without you."

She put out her arms as though to ward off a blow.

"No, no, Alban, don't try to move me. I can't. I must go. I can't live with you any more. It would be frightful. I can never forget. I must tell you the truth, I have only contempt for you and repulsion."

He sank down at her feet and tried to cling to her knees. With a gasp she sprang up and he buried his head in the empty chair. He cried painfully with sobs that tore his chest. The sound was horrible. The tears streamed from Anne's eyes and, putting her hands to her ears to shut out that dreadful, hysterical sobbing, blindly stumbling she rushed to the door and ran out.

The Four Dutchmen

THE Van Dorth Hotel at Singapore was far from grand. The bedrooms were dingy and the mosquito nets patched and darned; the bath-houses, all in a row and detached from the bedrooms, were dank and smelly. But it had character. The people who stayed there, masters of tramps whose round ended at Singapore, mining engineers out of a job and planters taking a holiday, to my mind bore a more romantic air than the smart folk, globe-trotters, government officials and their wives, wealthy merchants, who gave luncheon-parties at the Europe and played golf and danced and were fashionable. The Van Dorth had a billiard-room, with a table with a threadbare cloth, where ships' engineers and clerks in insurance offices played snooker. The dining-room was large and bare and silent. Dutch families on the way to Sumatra ate solidly through their dinner without exchanging a word with one another, and single gentlemen on a business trip from Batavia devoured a copious meal while they intently read their paper. On two days a week there was rijstafel and then a few residents of Singapore who had a fancy for this dish came for tiffin. The Van Dorth Hotel should have been a depressing place, but somehow it wasn't; its quaintness saved it. It had a faint aroma of something strange and half-forgotten. There was a scrap of garden facing the street where you could sit in the shade of trees and drink cold beer. In that crowded and busy city, though motors whizzed past and rickshaws passed continuously, the coolies' feet pattering on the road and their bells ringing, it had the remote peacefulness of a corner of

Holland. It was the third time I had stayed at the Van Dorth. I had been told about it first by the skipper of a Dutch tramp, the S.S. *Utrecht*, on which I had travelled from Merauke in New Guinea to Macassar. The journey took the best part of a month, since the ship stopped at a number of islands in the Malay Archipelago, the Aru and the Kei Islands, Banda-Neira, Amboina and others of which I have even forgotten the names, sometimes for an hour or two, sometimes for a day, to take on or discharge cargo. It was a charming, monotonous and diverting trip. When we dropped anchor the agent came out in his launch, and generally the Dutch Resident, and we gathered on deck under the awning and the captain ordered beer. The news of the island was exchanged for the news of the world. We brought papers and mail. If we were staying long enough the Resident asked us to dinner and, leaving the ship in charge of the second officer, we all (the captain, the chief officer, the engineer, the supercargo and I) piled into the launch and went ashore. We spent a merry evening. These little islands, one so like another, allured my fancy just because I knew that I should never see them again. It made them strangely unreal, and as we sailed away and they vanished into the sea and sky it was only by an effort of the imagination that I could persuade myself that they did not with my last glimpse of them cease to exist.

But there was nothing illusive, mysterious or fantastic about the captain, the chief officer, the chief engineer and the supercargo. Their solidity was amazing. They were the four fattest men I ever saw. At first I had great difficulty in telling them apart, for though one, the supercargo, was dark and the others were fair, they looked astonishingly alike. They were all big, with large round bare red faces, with large fat arms and large fat legs and large fat bellies. When they went ashore they buttoned up their stengah-shifters and then their great double chins bulged over the collars and they looked as though they would choke. But generally they wore them unbuttoned. They sweated freely and wiped their shiny faces with bandanas and vigorously fanned themselves with palm-leaf fans.

It was a treat to see them at tiffin. Their appetites were enormous. They had rijstafel every day, and each seemed to vie with the other how high he could pile his plate. They loved it hot and strong.

"In dis country you can't eat a ting onless it's tasty," said the skipper.

"De only way to keep yourself up in dis country is to eat hearty," said the chief.

They were the greatest friends, all four of them; they were like schoolboys together, playing absurd little pranks with one another. They knew each other's jokes by heart and no sooner did one of them start the familiar lines than he would splutter with laughter so violently, the heavy shaking laughter of the fat man, that he could not go on, and then the others began to laugh too. They rolled about in their chairs, and grew redder and redder, hotter and hotter, till the skipper shouted for beer, and each, gasping but happy, drank his bottle in one enchanted draught. They had been on this run together for five years and when, a little time before, the chief officer had been offered a ship of his own he refused it. He would not leave his companions. They had made up their minds that when the first of them retired they would all retire.

"All friends and a good ship. Good grub and good beer. Vot can a sensible man vant more?"

At first they were a little stand-offish with me. Although the ship had accommodation for half a dozen passengers, they did not often get any, and never one whom they did not know. I was a stranger and a foreigner. They liked their bit of fun and did not want anyone to interfere with it. But they were all of them very fond of bridge, and on occasion the chief and the engineer had duties that prevented one or the other from playing. They were willing to put up with me when they discovered that I was ready to make a fourth whenever I was wanted. Their bridge was as incredibly fantastic as they were. They played for infinitesimal stakes, five cents a hundred: they did not want to win one another's money, they said, it was the game they liked. But what a game! Each was wildly determined to play the hand and hardly one was dealt without at least a small slam being declared. The rule was that if you could get a peep at somebody else's cards you did and if you could get away with a revoke you told your partner when there was no danger it could be claimed and you both roared with laughter till the tears rolled down your fat cheeks. But if your partner had insisted on taking the bid away from you and had called a grand slam on five spades to the queen, whereas you were positive on your seven little diamonds you could have made it easily, you could always score him off by redoubling without a trick in your hand. He went down two or three thousand and the glasses on the table danced with the laughter that shook your opponents.

I could never remember their difficult Dutch names, but knowing them anonymously as it were, only by the duties they performed, as one knows the characters Pantaloon, Harlequin and Punchinello, of the old Italian comedy, added grotesquely to their drollery. The mere sight of them, all four together, set you laughing, and I think they got a good deal of amusement from the astonishment they caused in strangers. They boasted that they were the four most famous Dutchmen in the East Indies. To me not the least comic part of them was their serious side. Sometimes late at night, when they had given up all pretence of still wearing their uniforms, and one or the other of them lay by my side on a long chair in a pyjama jacket and a sarong, he would grow sentimental. The chief engineer, due to retire soon, was meditating marriage with a widow whom he had met when last he was home and spending the rest of his life in a little town with old red-brick houses on the shores of the Zuyder Zee. But the captain was very susceptible to the charms of the native girls and his thick English became almost unintelligible from emotion when he described to me the effect they had on him. One of these days he would buy himself a house on the hills in Java and marry a pretty little Javanese. They were so small and so gentle and they made no noise, and he would dress her in silk sarongs and give her gold chains to wear round her neck and gold bangles to put on her arms. But the chief mocked him.

"Silly all dat is. Silly. She goes mit all your friends and de house boys and everybody. By de time you retire, my dear, vot you'll vant vill be a nurse, not a vife."

"Me?" cried the skipper. "I shall want a vife ven I'm eighty!"

He had picked up a little thing last time the ship was at Macassar and as we approached that port he began to be all of a flutter. The chief officer shrugged fat and indulgent shoulders. The captain was always losing his head over one brazen hussy after another, but his passion never survived the interval between one stop at a port and the next, and then the chief was called in to smooth out the difficulties that ensued. And so it would be this time.

"De old man suffers from fatty degeneration of de heart. But so long as I'm dere to look after him not much harm comes of it. He vastes his money and dat's a pity, but as long as he's got it to vaste, why shouldn't he?"

The chief officer had a philosophic soul.

At Macassar then I disembarked, and bade farewell to my four fat friends.

"Make another journey with us," they said. "Come back next year or the year after. You'll find us all here just the same as ever."

A good many months had passed since then and I had wandered through more than one strange land. I had been to Bali and Java and Sumatra; I had been to Cambodia and Annam; and now, feeling as though I were home again, I sat in the garden of the Van Dorth Hotel. It was cool in the very early morning and having had breakfast I was looking at back numbers of the *Straits Times* to find out what had been happening in the world since last I had been within reach of papers. Nothing very much. Suddenly my eyes caught a headline: *The Utrecht Tragedy. Supercargo and Chief Engineer. Not Guilty*. I read the paragraph carelessly and then I sat up. The *Utrecht* was the ship of my four fat Dutchmen and apparently the supercargo and the chief engineer had been on trial for murder. It couldn't be my two fat friends. The names were given, but the names meant nothing to me. The trial had taken place in Batavia. No details were given in this paragraph; it was only a brief announcement that after the judges had considered the speeches of the prosecution and of the defence their verdict was as stated. I was astounded. It was incredible that the men I knew could have committed a murder. I could not find out who had been murdered. I looked through back numbers of the paper. Nothing.

I got up and went to the manager of the hotel, a genial Dutchman, who spoke admirable English, and showed him the paragraph.

"That's the ship I sailed on. I was in her for nearly a month. Surely these fellows aren't the men I knew. The men I knew were enormously fat."

"Yes, that's right," he answered. "They were celebrated all through the Dutch East Indies, the four fattest men in the service. It's been a terrible thing. It made a great sensation. And they were friends. I knew them all. The best fellows in the world."

"But what happened?"

He told me the story and answered my horrified questions. But there were things I wanted to know that he couldn't tell me. It was all confused. It was unbelievable. What actually had happened was only conjecture. Then someone claimed the manager's attention and I went back to the garden. It was getting hot now and I went up to my room. I was strangely shattered.

It appeared that on one of the trips the captain took with him a Malay girl that he had been carrying on with and I wondered if it was the one he had been so eager to see when I was on board. The other three had been against her coming – what did they want with a woman in the ship? It would spoil everything – but the captain insisted and she came. I think they were all jealous of her. On that journey they didn't have the fun they generally had. When they wanted to play bridge the skipper was dallying with the girl in his cabin; when they touched at a port and went ashore the time seemed long to him till he could get back to her. He was crazy about her. It was the end of all their larks. The chief officer was more bitter against her than anybody: he was the captain's particular chum, they had been shipmates ever since they first came out from Holland; more than once high words passed between them on the subject of the captain's infatuation. Presently those old friends spoke to one another only when their duties demanded it. It was the end of the good fellowship that had so long obtained between the four fat men. Things went from bad to worse. There was a feeling among the junior officers that something untoward was pending. Uneasiness. Tension. Then one night the ship was aroused by the sound of a shot and the screams of the Malay girl. The supercargo and the chief engineer tumbled out of their bunks and they found the captain, a revolver in his hand, at the door of the chief officer's cabin. He pushed past them and went on deck. They entered and found the chief officer dead and the girl cowering behind the door. The captain had found them in bed together and had killed the chief. How he had discovered what was going on didn't seem to be known, nor what was the meaning of the intrigue. Had the chief induced the girl to come to his cabin in order to get back on the captain, or had she, knowing his ill-will and anxious to placate him, lured him to become her lover? It was a mystery that would never be solved. A dozen possible explanations flashed across my mind. While the engineer and the supercargo were in the cabin, horror-struck at the sight before them, another shot was heard. They knew at once what had happened. They rushed up the companion. The captain had gone to his cabin and blown his brains out. Then the story grew dark and enigmatic. Next morning the Malay girl was nowhere to be found and when the second officer, who had taken command of the ship, reported this to the supercargo, the supercargo said: "She's probably jumped overboard. It's the best thing she could have done. Good riddance to bad rubbish." But one of the sailors on the watch, just before dawn, had seen the supercargo and the chief engineer carry something up on deck, a bulky package, about the size of a native woman, look about them to see that they were unobserved, and drop it overboard; and it was said all over the ship that these two to avenge their friends had sought the girl out in her cabin and strangled her and flung her body into the sea. When the ship arrived at Macassar they were arrested and taken to Batavia to be tried for murder. The evidence was flimsy and they were acquitted. But all through the East Indies they knew that the supercargo and the chief engineer had executed justice on the trollop who had caused the death of the two men they loved.

And thus ended the comic and celebrated friendship of the four fat Dutchmen.

P. & O.

Mrs. Hamlyn lay on her long chair and lazily watched the passengers come along the gangway. The ship had reached Singapore in the night, and since dawn had been taking on cargo; the winches had been grinding away all day, but by now her ears were accustomed to their insistent clamour. She had lunched at the Europe, and for lack of anything better to do had driven in a rickshaw through the gay, multitudinous streets of the city. Singapore is the meeting-place of many races. The Malays, though natives of the soil, dwell uneasily in towns, and are few; and it is the Chinese, supple, alert and industrious, who throng the streets; the dark-skinned Tamils walk on their silent, naked feet, as though they were but brief sojourners in a strange land, but the Bengalis, sleek and prosperous, are easy in their surroundings, and self-assured; the sly and obsequious Japanese seem busy with pressing and secret affairs; and the English in their topees and white ducks, speeding past in motor-cars or at leisure in their rickshaws, wear a nonchalant and careless air. The rulers of these teeming peoples take their authority with a smiling unconcern. And now, tired and hot, Mrs. Hamlyn waited for the ship to set out again on her long journey across the Indian Ocean.

She waved a rather large hand, for she was a big woman, to the doctor and Mrs. Linsell as they came on board. She had been on the ship since she left Yokohama, and had watched with acid amusement the intimacy which had sprung up between the two. Linsell was a naval officer who had been attached to the British

Embassy at Tokio, and she had wondered at the indifference with which he took the attentions that the doctor paid his wife. Two men came along the gangway, new passengers, and she amused herself by trying to discover from their demeanour whether they were single or married. Close by, a group of men were sitting together on rattan chairs, planters she judged by their khaki suits and wide-brimmed double felt hats, and they kept the deck-steward busy with their orders. They were talking loudly and laughing, for they had all drunk enough to make them somewhat foolishly hilarious, and they were evidently giving one of their number a send-off; but Mrs. Hamlyn could not tell which it was that was to be a fellow-passenger. The time was growing short. More passengers arrived, and then Mr. Jephson with dignity strolled up the gangway. He was a consul and was going home on leave. He had joined the ship at Shanghai and had immediately set about making himself agreeable to Mrs. Hamlyn. But just then she was disinclined for anything in the nature of a flirtation. She frowned as she thought of the reason which was taking her back to England. She would be spending Christmas at sea, far from anyone who cared two straws about her, and for a moment she felt a little twist at her heartstrings; it vexed her that a subject which she was so resolute to put away from her should so constantly intrude on her unwilling mind.

But a warning bell clanged loudly, and there was a general movement among the men who sat beside her.

"Well, if we don't want to be taken on we'd better be toddling," said one of them.

They rose and walked towards the gangway. Now that they were all shaking hands she saw who it was that they had come to see the last of. There was nothing very interesting about the man on whom Mrs. Hamlyn's eyes rested, but because she had nothing better to do she gave him more than a casual glance. He was a big fellow, well over six feet high, broad and stout; he was dressed in a bedraggled suit of khaki drill and his hat was battered and shabby. His friends left him, but they bandied chaff from the quay, and Mrs. Hamlyn noticed that he had a strong Irish brogue; his voice was full, loud and hearty.

Mrs. Linsell had gone below and the doctor came and sat down beside Mrs. Hamlyn. They told one another their small adventures of the day. The bell sounded again and presently the ship slid away from the wharf. The Irishman waved a last farewell to his friends, and then sauntered towards the chair on which he had left papers and magazines. He nodded to the doctor.

"Is that someone you know?" asked Mrs. Hamlyn.

"I was introduced to him at the club before tiffin. His name is Gallagher. He's a planter."

After the hubbub of the port and the noisy bustle of departure, the silence of the ship was marked and grateful. They steamed slowly past green-clad, rocky cliffs (the P. & O. anchorage was in a charming and secluded cove), and came out into the main harbour. Ships of all nations lay at anchor, a great multitude, passenger boats, tugs, lighters, tramps; and beyond, behind the breakwater, you saw the crowded masts, a bare straight forest, of the native junks. In the soft light of the evening the busy scene was strangely touched with mystery, and you felt that all those vessels, their activity for the moment suspended, waited for some event of a peculiar significance.

Mrs. Hamlyn was a bad sleeper and when the dawn broke she was in the habit of going on deck. It rested her troubled heart to watch the last faint stars fade before the encroaching day, and at that early hour the glassy sea had often an immobility which seemed to make all earthly sorrows of little consequence. The light was wan, and there was a pleasant shiver in the air. But next morning, when she went to the end of the promenade deck, she found that someone was up before her. It was Mr. Gallagher. He was watching the low coast of Sumatra which the sunrise like a magician seemed to call forth from the dark sea. She was startled and a little vexed, but before she could turn away he had seen her and nodded.

"Up early," he said. "Have a cigarette?"

He was in pyjamas and slippers. He took his case from his coat pocket and handed it to her. She hesitated. She had on nothing but a dressing-gown and a little lace cap which she had put over her tousled hair, and she knew that she must look a sight; but she had her reasons for scourging her soul.

"I suppose a woman of forty has no right to mind how she looks," she smiled, as though he must know what vain thoughts occupied her. She took the cigarette. "But you're up early too."

"I'm a planter. I've had to get up at five in the morning for so many years that I don't know how I'm going to get out of the habit."

"You'll not find it will make you very popular at home."

She saw his face better now that it was not shadowed by a hat. It was agreeable without being handsome. He was of course much too fat, and his features, which must have been good enough when he was a young man, were thickened. His skin was red and bloated. But his dark eyes were merry; and though he could not have been less than five and forty his hair was black and thick. He gave you an impression of great strength. He was a heavy, ungraceful, commonplace man, and Mrs. Hamlyn, except for the promiscuity of ship-board, would never have thought it worth while to talk to him.

"Are you going home on leave?" she hazarded.

"No, I'm going home for good."

His black eyes twinkled. He was of a communicative

turn, and before it was time for Mrs. Hamlyn to go below in order to have her bath he had told her a good deal about himself. He had been in the Federated Malay States for twenty-five years, and for the last ten had managed an estate in Selantan. It was a hundred miles from anything that could be described as civilisation and the life had been lonely; but he had made money; during the rubber boom he had done very well, and with an astuteness which was unexpected in a man who looked so happy-go-lucky he had invested his savings in government stock. Now that the slump had come he was prepared to retire.

"What part of Ireland do you come from?" asked Mrs. Hamlyn.

"Galway."

Mrs. Hamlyn had once motored through Ireland and she had a vague recollection of a sad and moody town with great stone warehouses, deserted and crumbling, which faced the melancholy sea. She had a sensation of greenness and of soft rain, of silence and of resignation. Was it here that Mr. Gallagher meant to spend the rest of his life? He spoke of it with boyish eagerness. The thought of his vitality in that grey world of shadows was so incongruous that Mrs. Hamlyn was intrigued.

"Does your family live there?" she asked.

"I've got no family. My mother and father are dead. So far as I know I haven't a relation in the world."

He had made all his plans, he had been making them for twenty-five years, and he was pleased to have someone to talk to of all these things that he had been obliged for so long only to talk to himself about. He meant to buy a house and he would keep a motor-car. He was going to breed horses. He didn't much care about shooting; he had shot a lot of big game during his first years in the F.M.S.; but now he had lost his zest. He didn't see why the beasts of the jungle should be killed; he had lived in the jungle so long. But he could hunt.

"Do you think I'm too heavy?" he asked.

Mrs. Hamlyn, smiling, looked him up and down with appraising eyes.

"You must weigh a ton," she said.

He laughed. The Irish horses were the best in the world, and he'd always kept pretty fit. You had a devil of a lot of walking exercise on a rubber estate and he'd played a good deal of tennis. He'd soon get thin in Ireland. Then he'd marry. Mrs. Hamlyn looked silently at the sea coloured now with the tenderness of the sunrise. She sighed.

"Was it easy to drag up all your roots? Is there no one you regret leaving behind? I should have thought after so many years, however much you'd looked forward to going home, when the time came at last to go it must have given you a pang."

"I was glad to get out. I was fed up. I never want to see the country again or anyone in it."

One or two early passengers now began to walk round the deck and Mrs. Hamlyn, remembering that she was scantily clad, went below.

During the next day or two she saw little of Mr. Gallagher, who passed his time in the smoking-room. Owing to a strike the ship was not touching at Colombo and the passengers settled down to a pleasant voyage across the Indian Ocean. They played deck games, they gossiped about one another, they flirted. The approach of Christmas gave them an occupation, for someone had suggested that there should be a fancy-dress dance on Christmas Day, and the ladies set about making their dresses. A meeting was held of the first-class passengers to decide whether the second-class passengers should be invited, and notwithstanding the heat the discussion was animated. The ladies said that the second-class passengers would only feel ill-at-ease. On Christmas Day it was to be expected that they would drink more than was good for them and unpleasantness might ensue.

Everyone who spoke insisted that there was in his (or her) mind no idea of class distinction, no one would be so snobbish as to think there was any difference between first and second-class passengers as far as that went, but it would really be kinder to the second-class passengers not to put them in a false position. They would enjoy themselves much more if they had a party of their own in the second-class cabin. On the other hand, no one wanted to hurt their feelings, and of course one had to be more democratic nowadays (this was in reply to the wife of a missionary in China who said she had travelled on the P. & O. for thirty-five years and she had never heard of the second-class passengers being invited to a dance in the first-class saloon) and even though they wouldn't enjoy it, they might like to come. Mr. Gallagher, dragged unwillingly from the card-table because it had been foreseen that the voting would be close, was asked his opinion by the consul. He was taking home in the second-class a man who had been employed on his estate. He raised his massive bulk from the couch on which he sat.

"As far as I'm concerned I've only got this to say: I've got the man who was looking after our engines with me. He's a rattling good fellow, and he's just as fit to come to your party as I am. But he won't come because I'm going to make him so drunk on Christmas Day that by six o'clock he'll be fit for nothing but to be put to bed."

Mr. Jephson, the consul, gave a distorted smile. On account of his official position, he had been chosen to preside at the meeting and he wished the matter to be taken seriously. He was a man who often said that if a thing was worth doing it was worth doing well.

"I gather from your observations," he said, not without acidity, "that the question before the meeting does not seem to you of great importance."

"I don't think it matters a tinker's curse," said Gallagher, with twinkling eyes.

Mrs. Hamlyn laughed. The scheme was at last devised to invite the second-class passengers, but to go to the captain privily and point out to him the advisability of withholding his consent to their coming into the first-class saloon. It was on the evening of the day on which this happened that Mrs. Hamlyn, having dressed for dinner, came on deck at the same time as Mr. Gallagher.

"Just in time for a cocktail, Mrs. Hamlyn," he said jovially.

"I'd like one. To tell you the truth I need cheering up."

"Why?" he smiled.

Mrs. Hamlyn thought his smile attractive, but she did not want to answer his question.

"I told you the other morning," she answered cheerfully. "I'm forty."

"I never met a woman who insisted on the fact so much."

They went into the lounge and the Irishman ordered a dry Martini for her and a gin pahit for himself. He had lived too long in the East to drink anything else.

"You've got hiccups," said Mrs. Hamlyn.

"Yes, I've had them all the afternoon," he answered carelessly. "It's rather funny, they came on just as we got out of sight of land."

"I daresay they'll pass off after dinner."

They drank, the second bell rang, and they went into the dining-saloon.

"You don't play bridge?" he said, as they parted.

"No."

Mrs. Hamlyn did not notice that she saw nothing of Gallagher for two or three days. She was occupied with her own thoughts. They crowded upon her when she was sewing; they came between her and the novel with which she sought to cheat their insistence. She had hoped that as the ship took her further away from the scene of her unhappiness, the torment of her mind would be eased; but contrariwise, each day that brought her nearer England increased her distress. She looked forward with dismay to the bleak emptiness of the life that awaited her; and then, turning her exhausted wits from a prospect that made her flinch, she considered, as she had done she knew not how many times before, the situation from which she had fled.

She had been married for twenty years. It was a long time and of course she could not expect her husband to be still madly in love with her; she was not madly in love with him; but they were good friends and they understood one another. Their marriage, as marriages go, might very well have been looked upon as a success. Suddenly she discovered that he had fallen in love. She would not have objected to a flirtation, he had had those before, and she had chaffed him about them; he had not minded that, it somewhat flattered him, and they had laughed together at an inclination which was neither deep nor serious. But this was different. He was in love as passionately as a boy of eighteen. He was fifty-two. It was ridiculous. It was indecent. And he loved without sense or prudence: by the time the hideous fact was forced upon her all the foreigners in Yokohama knew it. After the first shock of astonished anger, for he was the last man from whom such a folly might have been expected, she tried to persuade herself that she could have understood, and so have forgiven, if he had fallen in love with a girl. Middle-aged men often make fools of themselves with flappers, and after twenty years in the Far East she knew that the fifties were the dangerous age for men. But he had no excuse. He was in love with a woman eight years older than herself. It was grotesque, and it made her, his wife, perfectly absurd. Dorothy Lacom was hard on fifty. He had known her for eighteen years, for Lacom, like her own husband, was a silk merchant in Yokohama. Year in, year out, they had seen one another three or four times a week, and once, when they happened to be in England together, had shared a house at the sea-side. But nothing! Not till a year ago had there been anything between them but a chaffing friendship. It was incredible. Of course Dorothy was a handsome woman; she had a good figure, over-developed, perhaps, but still comely; with bold black eyes and a red mouth and lovely hair; but all that she had had years before. She was forty-eight. Forty-eight!

Mrs. Hamlyn tackled her husband at once. At first he swore that there was not a word of truth in what she accused him of, but she had her proofs; he grew sulky; and at last he admitted what he could no longer deny. Then he said an astonishing thing.

"Why should you care?" he asked.

It maddened her. She answered him with angry scorn. She was voluble, finding in the bitterness of her heart wounding things to say. He listened to her quietly.

"I've not been such a bad husband to you for the twenty years we've been married. For a long time now we've only been friends. I have a great affection for you, and this hasn't altered it in the very smallest degree. I'm giving Dorothy nothing that I take away from you."

"But what have you to complain of in me?"

"Nothing. No man could want a better wife."

"How can you say that when you have the heart to treat me so cruelly?"

"I don't want to be cruel to you. I can't help myself."

"But what on earth made you fall in love with her?"

"How can I tell? You don't think I wanted to, do you?"

"Couldn't you have resisted?"

"I tried. I think we both tried."

"You talk as though you were twenty. Why, you're both middle-aged people. She's eight years older than I am. It makes me look such a perfect fool."

He did not answer. She did not know what emotions seethed in her heart. Was it jealousy that seemed to clutch at her throat, anger, or was it merely wounded pride?

"I'm not going to let it go on. If only you and she were concerned I would divorce you, but there's her husband, and then there are the children. Good heavens, does it occur to you that if they were girls instead of boys she might be a grandmother by now?"

"Easily."

"What a mercy that we have no children!"

He put out an affectionate hand as though to caress her, but she drew back with horror.

"You've made me the laughing-stock of all my friends. For all our sakes I'm willing to hold my tongue, but only on the condition that everything stops now, at once, and for ever."

He looked down and played reflectively with a Japanese knick-knack that was on the table.

"I'll tell Dorothy what you say," he replied at last.

She gave him a little bow, silently, and walked past him out of the room. She was too angry to observe that she was somewhat melodramatic.

She waited for him to tell her the result of his interview with Dorothy Lacom, but he made no further reference to the scene. He was quiet, polite and silent; and at last she was obliged to ask him.

"Have you forgotten what I said to you the other day?" she inquired, frigidly.

"No. I talked to Dorothy. She wished me to tell you that she is desperately sorry that she has caused you so much pain. She would like to come and see you, but she is afraid you wouldn't like it."

"What decision have you come to?"

He hesitated. He was very grave, but his voice trembled a little.

"I'm afraid there's no use in our making a promise

we shouldn't be able to keep."

"That settles it then," she answered.

"I think I should tell you that if you brought an action for divorce we should have to contest it. You would find it impossible to get the necessary evidence and you would lose your case."

"I wasn't thinking of doing that. I shall go back to England and consult a lawyer. Nowadays these things can be managed fairly easily, and I shall throw myself on your generosity. I dare say you will enable me to get my freedom without bringing Dorothy Lacom into the matter."

He sighed.

"It's an awful muddle, isn't it? I don't want you to divorce me, but of course I'll do anything I can to meet your wishes."

"What on earth do you expect me to do?" she cried, her anger rising again. "Do you expect me to sit still and be made a damned fool of?"

"I'm awfully sorry to put you in a humiliating position." He looked at her with harassed eyes. "I'm quite sure we didn't want to fall in love with one another. We're both of us very conscious of our age. Dorothy, as you say, is old enough to be a grandmother and I'm a baldish, stoutish gentleman of fifty-two. When you fall in love at twenty you think your love will last for ever, but at fifty you know so much, about life and about love, and you know that it will last so short a time." His voice was low and rueful. It was as though before his mind's eye he saw the sadness of autumn and the leaves falling from the trees. He looked at her gravely. "And at that age you feel that you can't afford to throw away the chance of happiness which a freakish destiny has given you. In five years it will certainly be over, and perhaps in six months. Life is rather drab and grey, and happiness is so rare. We shall be dead so long."

It gave Mrs. Hamlyn a bitter sensation of pain to

hear her husband, a matter-of-fact and practical man, speak in a strain which was quite new to her. He had gained on a sudden a wistful and tragic personality of which she knew nothing. The twenty years during which they had lived together had no power over him and she was helpless in face of his determination. She could do nothing but go, and now, resentfully determined to get the divorce with which she had threatened him, she was on her way to England.

The smooth sea, upon which the sun beat down so that it shone like a sheet of glass, was as empty and hostile as life in which there was no place for her. For three days no other craft had broken in upon the solitariness of that expanse. Now and again its even surface was scattered for the twinkling of an eye by the scurry of flying fish. The heat was so great that even the most energetic of passengers had given up deck games, and now (it was after luncheon) such as were not resting in their cabins lay about on chairs. Linsell strolled towards her and sat down.

"Where's Mrs. Linsell?" asked Mrs. Hamlyn.

"Oh, I don't know. She's about somewhere."

His indifference exasperated her. Was it possible that he did not see that his wife and the surgeon were falling in love with one another? Yet, not so very long ago, he must have cared. Their marriage had been romantic. They had become engaged when Mrs. Linsell was still at school and he little more than a boy. They must have been a charming, handsome pair, and their youth and their mutual love must have been touching. And now, after so short a time, they were tired of one another. It was heartbreaking. What had her husband said?

"I suppose you're going to live in London when you get home?" asked Linsell lazily, for something to say.

"I suppose so," said Mrs. Hamlyn.

It was hard to reconcile herself to the fact that she had nowhere to go, and where she lived mattered not in the least to anyone alive. Some association of ideas made her think of Gallagher. She envied the eagerness with which he was returning to his native land, and she was touched, and at the same time amused, when she remembered the exuberant imagination he showed in describing the house he meant to live in and the wife he meant to marry. Her friends in Yokohama, apprised in confidence of her determination to divorce her husband, had assured her that she would marry again. She did not much want to enter a second time upon a state which had once so disappointed her, and besides, most men would think twice before they suggested marriage to a woman of forty. Mr. Gallagher wanted a buxom young person.

"Where is Mr. Gallagher?" she asked the submissive Linsell. "I haven't seen him for the last day or two."

"Didn't you know? He's ill."

"Poor thing. What's the matter with him?"

"He's got hiccups."

Mrs. Hamlyn laughed.

"Hiccups don't make one ill, do they?"

"The surgeon is rather worried. He's tried all sorts of things, but he can't stop them."

"How very odd."

She thought no more about it, but next morning, chancing upon the surgeon, she asked him how Mr. Gallagher was. She was surprised to see his boyish, cheerful face darken and grow perplexed.

"I'm afraid he's very bad, poor chap."

"With hiccups?" she cried in amazement.

It was a disorder that really it was impossible to take seriously.

"You see, he can't keep any food down. He can't sleep. He's fearfully exhausted. I've tried everything I can think of." He hesitated. "Unless I can stop them soon – I don't quite know what'll happen."

Mrs. Hamlyn was startled.

"But he's so strong. He seemed so full of vitality."

"I wish you could see him now."

"Would he like me to go and see him?"

"Come along."

Gallagher had been moved from his cabin into the ship's hospital, and as they approached it they heard a loud hiccup. The sound, perhaps owing to its connection with insobriety, had in it something ludicrous. But Gallagher's appearance gave Mrs. Hamlyn a shock. He had lost flesh and the skin hung about his neck in loose folds; under the sunburn his face was pale. His eyes, before, full of fun and laughter, were haggard and tormented. His great body was shaken incessantly by the hiccups and now there was nothing ludicrous in the sound; to Mrs. Hamlyn, for no reason that she knew, it seemed strangely terrifying. He smiled when she came in.

"I'm sorry to see you like this," she said.

"I shan't die of it, you know," he gasped. "I shall reach the green shores of Erin all right."

There was a man sitting beside him and he rose as they entered.

"This is Mr. Pryce," said the surgeon. "He was in charge of the machinery on Mr. Gallagher's estate."

Mrs. Hamlyn nodded. This was the second-class passenger to whom Gallagher had referred when they had discussed the party which was to be given on Christmas Day. He was a very small man, but sturdy, with a pleasantly impudent countenance and an air of self-assurance.

"Are you glad to be going home?" asked Mrs. Hamlyn.

"You bet I am, lady," he answered.

The intonation of the few words told Mrs. Hamlyn that he was a cockney and, recognising the cheerful, sensible, good-humoured and careless type, her heart warmed to him.

"You're not Irish?" she smiled.

"Not me, miss. London's my 'ome and I shan't be sorry to see it again, I can tell you."

Mrs. Hamlyn never thought it offensive to be called miss.

"Well, sir, I'll be getting along," he said to Gallagher, with the beginning of a gesture as though he were going to touch a cap which he hadn't got on.

Mrs. Hamlyn asked the sick man whether she could do anything for him and in a minute or two left him with the doctor. The little cockney was waiting outside the door.

"Can I speak to you a minute or two, miss?" he asked.

"Of course."

The hospital cabin was aft and they stood, leaning against the rail, and looked down on the well-deck where lascars and stewards off duty were lounging about on the covered hatches.

"I don't know exactly 'ow to begin," said Pryce, uncertainly, a serious look strangely changing his lively, puckered face. "I've been with Mr. Gallagher for four years now and a better gentleman you wouldn't find in a week of Sundays."

He hesitated again.

"I don't like it and that's the truth."

"What don't you like?"

"Well, if you ask me 'e's for it, and the doctor don't know it. I told 'im, but 'e won't listen to a word I say."

"You mustn't be too depressed, Mr. Pryce. Of course the doctor's young, but I think he's quite clever, and people don't die of hiccups, you know. I'm sure Mr. Gallagher will be all right in a day or two."

"You know when it come on? Just as we was out of sight of land. She said 'e'd never see 'is 'ome."

Mrs. Hamlyn turned and faced him. She stood a good three inches taller than he.

"What do you mean?"

"My belief is, it's a spell been put on 'im, if you understand what I mean. Medicine's going to do 'im no good. You don't know them Malay women like what I do."

For a moment Mrs. Hamlyn was startled, and because she was startled she shrugged her shoulders and laughed.

"Oh, Mr. Pryce, that's nonsense."

"That's what the doctor said when I told 'im But you mark my words, 'e'll die before we see land again."

The man was so serious that Mrs. Hamlyn, vaguely uneasy, was against her will impressed.

"Why should anyone cast a spell on Mr. Gallagher?" she asked.

"Well, it's a bit awkward speaking' of it to a lady."

"Please tell me."

Pryce was so embarrassed that at another time Mrs. Hamlyn would have had difficulty in concealing her amusement.

"Mr. Gallagher's lived a long time up-country, if you understand what I mean, and of course it's lonely, and you know what men are, miss."

"I've been married for twenty years," she replied, smiling.

"I beg your pardon, ma'am. The fact is he had a Malay girl living with him. I don't know 'ow long, ten or twelve years, I think. Well, when 'e made up 'is mind to come 'ome for good she didn't say nothing. She just sat there. He thought she'd carry on no end, but she didn't. Of course 'e provided for 'er all right, 'e gave 'er a little 'ouse for herself, an' 'e fixed it up so as so much should be paid 'er every month. 'E wasn't mean, I will say that for 'im, an' she knew all along as 'e'd be going some time. She didn't cry or anything. When 'e packed up all 'is things and sent them off, she just sat there an' watched 'em go. And when 'e sold 'is furniture to the Chinks she never said a word. He'd give 'er all she wanted. And when it was time for 'im to go so as to catch the boat she just kep' on sitting on the steps of the bungalow, you know, and she just looked an' said nothing. He wanted to say good-bye to 'er, same as anyone would, an', would you believe it? she never even moved. 'Aren't you going to say good-by to me,' he says. A rare funny look come over 'er face. And do you know what she says? 'You go,' she says; they 'ave a funny way of talking, them natives, not like we 'ave, 'you go,' she says, 'but I tell you that you will never come to your own country. When the land sinks into the sea, death will come upon you, an' before them as goes with you sees the land again, death will have took you.' It gave me quite a turn."

"What did Mr. Gallagher say?" asked Mrs. Hamlyn.

"Oh, well, you know what 'e is. He just laughed. 'Always merry and bright,' 'e says and 'e jumps into the motor, an' off we go."

Mrs. Hamlyn saw the bright and sunny road that ran through the rubber estates, with their trim green trees, carefully spaced, and their silence, and then wound its way up hill and down through the tangled jungle. The car raced on, driven by a reckless Malay, with its white passengers, past Malay houses that stood away from the road among the coconut trees, sequestered and taciturn, and through busy villages where the market-place was crowded with dark-skinned little people in gay sarongs. Then towards evening it reached the trim, modern town, with its clubs and its golf links, its well-ordered rest-house, its white people, and its railway-station, from which the two men could take the train to Singapore. And the woman sat on the steps of the bungalow, empty till the new manager moved in, and watched the road down which the car had panted, watched the car as it sped on, and watched till at last it was lost in the shadow of the night.

"What was she like?" Mrs. Hamlyn asked.

"Oh, well, to my way of thinking them Malay

women are all very much alike, you know," Pryce answered. "Of course she wasn't so young any more, and you know what they are, them natives, they run to fat something terrible."

"Fat?"

The thought, absurdly enough, filled Mrs. Hamlyn with dismay.

"Mr. Gallagher was always one to do himself well, if you understand what I mean."

The idea of corpulence at once brought Mrs. Hamlyn back to common sense. She was impatient with herself because for an instant she had seemed to accept the little cockney's suggestion.

"It's perfectly absurd, Mr. Pryce. Fat women can't throw spells on people at a distance of a thousand miles. In fact life is very difficult for a fat woman anyway."

"You can laugh, miss, but unless something's done, you mark my words, the governor's for it. And medicine ain't goin' to save him, not white man's medicine."

"Pull yourself together, Mr. Pryce. This fat lady had no particular grievance against Mr. Gallagher. As these things are done in the East he seems to have treated her very well. Why should she wish him any harm?"

"We don't know 'ow they look at things. Why, a man can live there for twenty years with one them natives, and d'you think 'e knows what's goin' on in that black heart of hers? Not 'im!"

She could not smile at his melodramatic language, for his intensity was impressive. And she knew, if anyone did, that the hearts of men, whether their skins are yellow or white or brown, are incalculable.

"But even if she felt angry with him, even if she hated him and wanted to kill him, what could she do?" It was strange that Mrs. Hamlyn with her questions was trying now, unconsciously, to reassure herself. "There's no poison that could start working after six or seven days."

"I nver said it was poison."

"I'm sorry, Mr. Pryce," she smiled, "but I'm not going to believe in a magic spell, you know."

"You've lived in the East?"

"Off and on for twenty years."

"Well, if you can say what they can do and what they can't, it's more than I can." He clenched his fist and beat it on the rail with sudden, angry violence. "I'm fed up with the bloody country. It's got on my nerves, that's what it is. We're no match for them, us white men, and that's a fact. If you'll excuse me I think I'll go an' 'ave a tiddley. I've got the jumps."

He nodded abruptly and left her. Mrs. Hamlyn watched him, a sturdy, shuffling little man in shabby khaki, slither down the companion into the waist of the ship, walk across it with bent head, and disappear into the second-class saloon. She did not know why he left with her a vague uneasiness. She could not get out of her mind that picture of a stout woman, no longer young, in a sarong, a coloured jacket and gold ornaments, who sat on the steps of a bungalow looking at an empty road. Her heavy face was painted, but in her large, tearless eyes there was no expression. The men who drove in the car were like schoolboys going home for the holidays. Gallagher gave a sigh of relief. In the early morning, under the bright sky, his spirits bubbled. The future was like a sunny road that wandered through a wide-flung, wooded plain.

Later in the day Mrs. Hamlyn asked the doctor how his patient did. The doctor shook his head.

"I'm done. I'm at the end of my tether." He frowned unhappily. "It's rotten luck, striking a case like this. It would be bad enough at home, but on board ship..."

He was an Edinburgh man, but recently qualified, and he was taking this voyage as a holiday before settling down to practice. He felt himself aggrieved. He wanted to have a good time and, faced with this mysterious illness, he was worried to death. Of course he was inexperienced, but he was doing everything that could be done and it exasperated him to suspect that the passengers thought him an ignorant fool.

"Have you heard what Mr. Pryce thinks?" asked Mrs. Hamlyn.

"I never heard such rot. I told the captain and he's right up in the air. He doesn't want it talked about. He thinks it'll upset the passengers."

"I'll be as silent as the grave."

The surgeon looked at her sharply.

"Of course you don't believe that there can be any truth in nonsense of that sort?" he asked.

"Of course not." She looked out at the sea, which shone, blue and oily and still, all round them. "I've lived in the East a long time," she added. "Strange things happen there."

"This is getting on my nerves," said the doctor.

Near them two little Japanese gentlemen were playing deck quoits. They were trim and neat in their tennis shirts, white trousers and buckram shoes. They looked very European, they even called the score to one another in English, and yet somehow to look at them filled Mrs. Hamlyn at that moment with a vague disquiet. Because they seemed to wear so easily a disguise there was about them something sinister. Her nerves too were on edge.

And presently, no one quite knew how, the notion spread through the ship that Gallagher was bewitched. While the ladies sat about on their deck-chairs, stitching away at the costumes they were making for the fancy-dress party on Christmas Day, they gossiped about it in undertones, and the men in the smoking-room talked of it over their cocktails. A good many of the passengers had lived long in the East and from the recesses of their memory they produced strange and inexplicable stories. Of course it was absurd to think seriously that Gallagher was suffering from a malignant spell, such things were impossible, and yet this and that was a fact and no one had been able to explain it. The doctor had to confess that he could suggest no cause for Gallagher's condition, he was able to give a physiological explanation, but why terrible spasms should have suddenly assailed him he did not say. Feeling vaguely to blame, he tried to defend himself.

"Why, it's the sort of case you might never come across in the whole of your practice," he said. "It's rotten luck."

He was in wireless communication with passing ships, and suggestions for treatment came from here and there.

"I've tried everything they tell me," he said irritably. "The doctor of the Japanese boat advised adrenalin. How the devil does he expect me to have adrenalin in the middle of the Indian Ocean?"

There was something impressive in the thought of this ship speeding through a deserted sea, while to her from all parts came unseen messages. She seemed at that moment strangely alone and yet the centre of the world. In the lazaret the sick man, shaken by the cruel spasms, gasped for life. Then the passengers became conscious that the ship's course was altered, and they heard that the captain had made up his mind to put in at Aden. Gallagher was to be landed there and taken to the hospital, where he could have attention which on board was impossible. The chief engineer received orders to force his engines. The ship was an old one and she throbbed with the greater effort. The passengers had grown used to the sound and feel of her engines, and now the greater vibration shook their nerves with a new sensation. It would not pass into each one's unconsciousness, but beat on their sensibilities so that each felt a personal concern. And still the wide sea was empty of traffic, so that they seemed to traverse an empty world. And now the uneasiness which had descended upon the ship, but which no one had been willing to acknowledge, became a definite malaise. The passengers grew irritable, and people quarrelled over trifles which at another time would have seemed insignificant. Mr. Jephson made his hackneyed jokes, but no one any longer repaid him with a smile. The Linsells had an altercation, and Mrs. Linsell was heard late at night walking round the deck with her husband and uttering in a low, tense voice a stream of vehement reproaches. There was a violent scene in the smoking room one night over a game of bridge, and the reconciliation which followed it was attended with general intoxication. People talked little of Gallagher, but he was seldom absent from their thoughts. They examined the route map. The doctor said now that Gallagher could not live more than three or four days, and they discussed acrimoniously what was the shortest time in which Aden could be reached. What happened to him after he was landed was no affair of theirs; they did not want him to die on board.

Mrs. Hamlyn saw Gallagher every day. With the suddenness with which after tropical rain in the spring you seem to see the herbage grow before your very eyes, she saw him go to pieces. Already his skin hung loosely on his bones, and his double chin was like the wrinkled wattle of a turkey-cock. His cheeks were sunken. You saw now how large his frame was, and through the sheet under which he lay his bony structure was like the skeleton of a prehistoric giant. For the most part he lay with his eyes closed, torpid with morphia, but shaken still with terrible spasms, and when now and again he opened his eyes they were preternaturally large; they looked at you vaguely, perplexed and troubled, from the depths of their bony sockets. But when, emerging from his stupor, he recognised Mrs. Hamlyn, he forced a gallant smile to his lips.

"How are you, Mr. Gallagher?" she said.

"Getting along, getting along. I shall be all right when we get out of this confounded heat. Lord, how I look forward to a dip in the Atlantic. I'd give anything for a good long swim. I want to feel the cold grey sea of Galway beating against my chest."

Then the hiccup shook him from the crown of his head to the sole of his foot. Mr. Pryce and the stewardess shared the care of him. The little cockney's face wore no longer its look of impudent gaiety, but instead was sullen.

"The captain sent for me yesterday," he told Mrs. Hamlyn when they were alone. "He gave me a rare talking to."

"What about?"

"He said 'e wouldn't 'ave all this hoodoo stuff. He said it was frightening the passengers and I'd better keep a watch on me tongue or I'd 'ave 'im to reckon with. It's not my doing. I never said a word except to you and the doctor."

"It's all over the ship."

"I know it is, D'you think it's only me that's saying it? All them Lascars and the Chinese, they all know what's the matter with him. You don't think you can teach them much, do you? They know it ain't a natural illness."

Mrs. Hamlyn was silent. She knew through the amahs of some of the passengers that there was no one on the ship, except the whites, who doubted that the woman whom Gallagher had left in distant Selantan was killing him with her magic. All were convinced that as they sighted the barren rocks of Arabia his soul would be parted from his body.

"The captain says if he hears of me trying any hanky-panky he'll confine me to my cabin for the rest of the voyage," said Pryce, suddenly, a surly frown on his puckered face.

"What do you mean by hanky-panky?"

He looked at her for a moment fiercely as though she too were an object of the anger he felt against the captain.

"The doctor's tried every damned thing he knows, and he's wirelessed all over the place, and what good 'as 'e done? Tell me that. Can't 'e see the man's dying? There's only one way to save him now."

"What do you mean?"

"It's magic what's killing 'im, and it's only magic what'll save him. Oh, don't you say it can't be done. I've seen it with me own eyes." His voice rose, irritable and shrill. "I've seen a man dragged from the jaws of death, as you might say, when they got in a *pawang*, what we call a witch-doctor, an' 'e did 'is little tricks. I seen it with me own eyes, I tell you."

Mrs. Hamlyn did not speak. Pryce gave her a searching look.

"One of them Lascars on board, he's a witch-doctor same as the *pawang* thet we 'ave in the F.M.S. An' 'e says he'll do it. Only he must 'ave a live animal. A cock would do."

"What do you want a live animal for?" Mrs. Hamlyn asked, frowning a little.

The cockney looked at her with quick suspicion. "If you take my advice you won't know anything about it. But I tell you what, I'm going to leave no stone unturned to save my governor. An' if the captin 'ears of it and shuts me up in me cabin, well, let 'im."

At that moment Mrs. Linsell came up and Pryce with his quaint gesture of salute left them. Mrs. Linsell wanted Mrs. Hamlyn to fit the dress she had been making herself for the fancy-dress ball, and on the way down to the cabin she spoke to her anxiously of the possibility that Mr. Gallagher might die on Christmas Day. They could not possibly have the dance if he did. She had told the doctor that she would never speak to him again if this happened, and the doctor had promised her faithfully that he would keep the man alive over Christmas Day somehow.

"It would be nice for him, too," said Mrs. Linsell.

"For whom?" asked Mrs. Hamlyn.

"For poor Mr. Gallagher. Naturally no one likes to die on Christmas Day. Do they?"

"I don't really know," said Mrs. Hamlyn.

That night, after she had been asleep a little while, she awoke weeping. It dismayed her that she should cry in her sleep. It was as though then the weakness of the flesh mastered her, and, her will broken, she were defenceless against a natural sorrow. She turned over in her mind, as so often before, the details of the disaster which had so profoundly affected her; she repeated the conversations with her husband, wishing she had said this and blaming herself because she had said the other. She wished with all her heart that she had remained in comfortable ignorance of her husband's infatuation, and asked herself whether she would not have been wiser to pocket her pride and shut her eyes to the unwelcome truth. She was a woman of the world, and she knew too well how much more she lost in separating herself from her husband than his love; she lost the settled establishment and the assured position, the ample means and the support of a recognised background. She had known of many separated wives, living equivocally on smallish incomes, and knew how quickly their friends found them tiresome. And she was lonely. She was as lonely as the ship that throbbed her hasting way through an unpeopled sea, and lonely as the friendless man who lay dying in the ship's lazaret. Mrs. Hamlyn knew that her thoughts had got the better of her now and that she would not easily sleep again. It was very hot in her cabin. She looked at the time; it was between four and half-past; she must pass two mortal hours before broke the reassuring day.

She slipped into a kimono and went on deck. The night was sombre and although the sky was unclouded no stars were visible. Panting and shaking, the old ship under full steam lumbered through the darkness. The silence was uncanny. Mrs. Hamlyn with bare feet groped her way slowly along the deserted deck.

It was so black that she could see nothing. She came to the end of the promenade deck and leaned against the rail. Suddenly she started and her attention was fixed, for on the lower deck she caught a fitful glow. She leaned forward cautiously. It was a little fire, and she saw only the glow because the naked backs of men, crouched round, hid the flame. At the edge of the circle she divined, rather than saw, a stocky figure in pyjamas. The rest were natives, but this was a European. It must be Pryce and she guessed immediately that some dark ceremony of exorcism was in progress. Straining her ears she heard a low voice muttering a string of secret words. She began to tremble. She was aware that they were too intent upon their business to think that anyone was watching them, but she dared not move. Suddenly, rending the sultry silence of the night like a piece of silk violently torn in two, came the crowing of a cock. Mrs. Hamlyn almost shrieked. Mr. Pryce was trying to save the life of his friend and master by a sacrifice to the strange gods of the East. The voice went on, low and insistent. Then in the dark circle there was a movement, something was happening, she knew not what; there was a cluck-cluck from the cock, angry and frightened, and then a strange, indescribable sound; the magician was cutting the cock's throat; then silence; there were vague doings that she could not follow, and in a little while it looked as though someone were stamping out the fire. The figures she had dimly seen were dissolved in the night and all once more was still. She heard again the regular throbbing of the engines.

Mrs. Hamlyn stood still for a little while, strangely shaken, and then walked slowly along the deck. She found a chair and lay down in it. She was trembling still. She could only guess what had happened. She did not know how long she lay there, but at last she felt that the dawn was approaching. It was not yet day, and it was no longer night. Against the darkness of the sky she could now see the ship's rail. Then she saw a figure come towards her. It was a man in pyjamas.

"Who's that?" she cried nervously.

"Only the doctor," came a friendly voice.

"Oh! What are you doing here at this time of night?"

"I've been with Gallagher." He sat down beside her and lit a cigarette. "I've given him a good strong hypodermic and he's quiet now."

"Has he been very ill?"

"I thought he was going to pass out. I was watching him, and suddenly he started up on his bed and began to talk Malay. Of course I couldn't understand a thing. He kept on saying one word over and over again."

"Perhaps it was a name, a woman's name."

"He wanted to get out of bed. He's a damned powerful man even now. By George, I had a struggle with him. I was afraid he'd throw himself overboard. He seemed to think someone was calling him."

"When was that?" asked Mrs. Hamlyn, slowly.

"Between four and half-past. Why?"

"Nothing."

She shuddered.

Later in the morning when the ship's life was set upon its daily round, Mrs. Hamlyn passed Pryce on the deck, but he gave her a brief greeting and walked on with quickly averted gaze. He looked tired and overwrought. Mrs. Hamlyn thought again of that fat woman, with golden ornaments in her thick, black hair, who sat on the steps of the deserted bungalow and looked at the road which ran through the trim lines of the rubber trees.

It was fearfully hot. She knew now why the night had been so dark. The sky was no longer blue, but a dead, level white; its surface was too even to give the effect of cloud; it was as though in the upper air the heat hung like a pall. There was no breeze and the sea, as colourless as the sky, was smooth and shining like the dye in a dyer's vat. The passengers were listless; when they walked round the deck they panted, and beads of sweat broke out on their foreheads. They spoke in undertones. Something uncanny and disquieting brooded over the ship, and they could not bring themselves to laugh. A feeling of resentment arose in their hearts; they were alive and well, and it exasperated them that, so near, a man should be dying and by the fact (which was after all no concern of theirs) so mysteriously affect them. A planter in the smoking-room over a gin sling said brutally what most of them felt, though none had confessed.

"Well, if he's going to peg out," he said, "I wish he'd hurry up and get it over. It gives me the creeps."

The day was interminable. Mrs. Hamlyn was thankful when the dinner hour arrived. So much time, at all events, was passed. She sat at the doctor's table.

"When do we reach Aden?" she asked.

"Some time to-morrow. The captain says we shall sight land between five and six in the morning."

She gave him a sharp look. He stared at her for a moment, then dropped his eyes and reddened. He remembered that the woman, the fat woman sitting on the bungalow steps, had said that Gallagher would never see the land. Mrs. Hamlyn wondered whether he, the sceptical, matter-of-fact young doctor, was wavering at last. He frowned a little and then, as though he sought to pull himself together, looked at her once more.

"I shan't be sorry to hand over my patient to the hospital people at Aden, I can tell you," he said.

Next day was Christmas Eve. When Mrs. Hamlyn awoke from a troubled sleep the dawn was breaking. She looked out of her port-hole and saw that the sky was clear and silvery; during the night the haze had melted, and the morning was brilliant. With a lighter heart she went on deck. She walked as far forward as she could go. A late star twinkled palely close to the horizon.

There was a shimmer on the sea as though a loitering breeze passed playful fingers over its surface. The light was wonderfully soft, tenuous like a budding wood in spring, and crystalline so that it reminded you of the bubbling of water in a mountain brook. She turned to look at the sun rising rosy in the east, and saw coming towards her the doctor. He wore his uniform; he had not been to bed all night; he was dishevelled and he walked, with bowed shoulders, as though he were dog-tired. She knew at once that Gallagher was dead. When he came up to her she saw that he was crying. He looked so young then that her heart went out to him. She took his hand.

"You poor dear," she said. "You're tired out."

"I did all I could," he said. "I wanted so awfully to save him."

His voice shook and she saw that he was almost hysterical.

"When did he die?" she asked.

He closed his eyes, trying to control himself, and his lips trembled.

"A few minutes ago."

Mrs. Hamlyn sighed. She found nothing to say. Her gaze wandered across the calm, dispassionate and ageless sea. It stretched on all sides of them as infinite as human sorrow. But on a sudden her eyes were held, for there, ahead of them, on the horizon was something which looked like a precipitous and massy cloud. But its outline was too sharp to be a cloud's. She touched the doctor on the arm.

"What's that?"

He looked at it for a moment and under his sunburn she saw him grow white.

"Land."

Once more Mrs. Hamlyn thought of the fat Malay woman who sat silent on the steps of Gallagher's bungalow. Did she know?

They buried him when the sun was high in the heavens. They stood on the lower deck and on the hatches, the first- and second-class passengers, the white stewards and the European officers. The missionary read the burial service.

"Man that is born of a woman hath but a short time to live, and is full of misery. He cometh up, and is cut down, like a flower; he fleeth as it were a shadow, and never continueth in one stay."

Pryce looked down at the deck with knit brows. His teeth were tight clenched. He did not grieve, for his heart was hot with anger. The doctor and the consul stood side by side. The consul bore to a nicety the expression of an official regret, but the doctor, clean-shaven now, in his neat fresh uniform and his gold braid, was pale and harassed. From him Mrs. Hamlyn's eyes wandered to Mrs. Linsell. She was pressed against her husband, weeping, and he was holding her hand tenderly. Mrs. Hamlyn did not know why this sight singularly affected her. At that moment of grief, her nerves distraught, the little woman went by instinct to the protection and support of her husband. But then Mrs. Hamlyn felt a little shudder pass through her and she fixed her eyes on the seams in the deck, for she did not want to see what was toward. There was a pause in the reading. There were various movements. One of the officers gave an order. The missionary's voice continued.

"Forasmuch as it has pleased Almighty God of his great mercy to take unto himself the soul of our dear brother here departed: we therefore commend his body to the deep, to be turned into corruption, looking for the resurrection of the body when the sea shall give up its dead."

Mrs. Hamlyn felt the hot tears flow down her cheeks. There was a dull splash. The missionary's voice went on.

When the service was finished the passengers scattered; the second-class passengers returned to their quarters and a bell rang to summon them to luncheon. But the first-class passengers sauntered aimlessly about the promenade deck. Most of the men made for the smoking-room and sought to cheer themselves with whiskies and sodas and with gin slings. But the consul put up a notice on the board outside the dining-saloon summoning the passengers to a meeting. Most of them had an idea for what purpose it was called, and at the appointed hour they assembled. They were more cheerful than they had been for a week and they chattered with a gaiety which was only subdued by a mannerly reserve. The consul, an eyeglass in his eye, said that he had gathered them together to discuss the question of the fancy-dress dance on the following day. He knew they all had the deepest sympathy for Mr. Gallagher and he would have proposed that they should combine to send an appropriate message to the deceased's relatives; but his papers had been examined by the purser and no trace could be found of any relative or friend with whom it was possible to communicate. The late Mr. Gallagher appeared to be quite alone in the world. Meanwhile he (the consul) ventured to offer his sincere sympathy to the doctor, who, he was quite sure, had done everything that was possible in the circumstances.

"Hear, hear," said the passengers.

They had all passed through a very trying time, proceeded the consul, and to some it might seem that it would be more respectful to the deceased's memory if the fancy-dress ball were postponed till New Year's Eve. This, however, he told them frankly was not his view, and he was convinced that Mr. Gallagher himself would not have wished it. Of course it was a question for the majority to decide. The doctor got up and thanked the consul and the passengers for the kind things that had been said of him, it had of course been a very trying time, but he was authorised by the captain to say that the captain expressly wished all the festivities to be carried out on Christmas Day as though nothing had happened. He (the doctor) told them in confidence that the captain felt the passengers had got into a rather morbid state, and thought it would do them all good if they had a jolly good time on Christmas Day. Then the missionary's wife rose and said they mustn't think only of themselves; it had been arranged by the Entertainment Committee that there should be a Christmas Tree for the children, immediately after the first-class passengers' dinner, and the children had been looking forward to seeing everyone in fancy-dress; it would be too bad to disappoint them; she yielded to no one in her respect for the dead, and she sympathised with anyone who felt too sad to think of dancing just then, her own heart was very heavy, but she did feel it would be merely selfish to give way to a feeling which could do no good to anyone. Let them think of the little ones. This very much impressed the passengers. They wanted to forget the brooding terror which had hung over the boat for so many days, they were alive and they wanted to enjoy themselves; but they had an uneasy notion that it would be decent to exhibit a certain grief. It was quite another matter if they could do as they wished from altruistic motives. When the consul called for a show of hands everyone, but Mrs. Hamlyn and one old lady who was rheumatic, held up an eager arm.

"The ayes have it," said the consul. "And I venture to congratulate the meeting on a very sensible decision."

It was just going to break up when one of the planters got on his feet and said he wished to offer a suggestion. Under the circumstances didn't they all think it would be as well to invite the second-class passengers? They had all come to the funeral that morning. The missionary jumped up and seconded the motion. The events of the last few days had drawn them all together, he said, and in the presence of death all men were equal. The consul again addressed them. This matter had been discussed at a previous meeting, and the conclusion had been reached that it would be pleasanter for the second-class passengers to have their own party, but circumstances alter cases, and he was distinctly of opinion that their previous decision should be reversed.

"Hear, hear," said the passengers.

A wave of democratic feeling swept over them and the motion was carried by acclamation. They separated light-heartedly, they felt charitable and kindly. Everyone stood everyone else drinks in the smoking-room.

And so, on the following evening, Mrs. Hamlyn put on her fancy-dress. She had no heart for the gaiety before her, and for a moment had thought of feigning illness, but she knew no one would believe her, and was afraid to be thought affected. She was dressed as Carmen and she could not resist the vanity of making herself as attractive as possible. She darkened her eyelashes and rouged her cheeks. The costume suited her. When the bugle sounded and she went into the saloon she was received with flattering surprise. The consul (always a humorist) was dressed as a ballet-girl and was greeted with shouts of delighted laughter. The missionary and his wife, self-conscious but pleased with themselves, were very grand as Manchus. Mrs. Linsell, as Columbine, showed all that was possible of her very pretty legs. Her husband was an Arab sheik and the doctor was a Malay sultan.

A subscription had been collected to provide champagne at dinner and the meal was hilarious. The company had provided crackers in which were paper hats of various shapes and these the passengers put on. There were paper streamers too which they threw at one another and little balloons which they beat from one to the other across the room. They laughed and shouted. They were very gay. No one could say that they were not having a good time. As soon as dinner was finished they went into the saloon, where the Christmas Tree, with candles lit, was ready, and the children were brought in, shrieking with delight, and given presents. Then the dance began. The second-class passengers stood about shyly round the part of the deck reserved for dancing and occasionally danced with one another.

"I'm glad we had them," said the consul, dancing with Mrs. Hamlyn. "I'm all for democracy, and I think they're very sensible to keep themselves to themselves."

But she noticed that Pryce was not to be seen, and when an opportunity presented asked one of the second-class passengers where he was.

"Blind to the world," was the answer. "We put him to bed in the afternoon and locked him up in his cabin."

The consul claimed her for another dance. He was very facetious. Suddenly Mrs. Hamlyn felt that she could not bear it any more, the noise of the amateur band, the consul's jokes, the gaiety of the dancers. She knew not why, but the merriment of those people passing on their ship through the night and the solitary sea affected her on a sudden with horror. When the consul released her she slipped away and, with a look to see that no one had noticed her, ascended the companion to the boat deck. Here everything was in darkness. She walked softly to a spot where she knew she would be safe from all intrusion. But she heard a faint laugh and she caught sight in a hidden corner of a Columbine and a Malay sultan. Mrs. Linsell and the doctor had resumed already the flirtation which the death of Gallagher had interrupted.

Already all those people had put out of their minds with a kind of ferocity the thought of that poor lonely man who had so strangely died in their midst. They felt no compassion for him, but resentment rather, because on his account they had been ill-at-ease. They seized upon life avidly. They made their jokes, they flirted, they gossiped. Mrs. Hamlyn remembered what the consul had said, that among Mr. Gallagher's papers no letters could be found, not the name of a single friend to whom the news of his death might be sent, and she knew not why this seemed to her unbearably tragic. There was something mysterious in a man who could pass through the world in such solitariness. When she remembered how he had come on deck in Singapore, so short a while since, in such rude health, full of vitality, and his arrogant plans for the future, she was seized with dismay. Those words of the burial service filled her with a solemn awe: *Man that is born of a woman hath but a short time to live, and is full of misery. He cometh up, and is cut down, like a flower*...Year in, year out, he had made his plans for the future, he wanted to live so much and he had so much to live for, and then just when he stretched out his hand – oh, it was pitiful; it made all the other distresses of the world of small account. Death with its mystery was the only thing that really mattered. Mrs. Hamlyn leaned over the rail and looked at the starry sky. Why did people make themselves unhappy? Let them weep for the death of those they loved, death was terrible always, but for the rest, was it worth while to be wretched, to harbour malice, to be vain and uncharitable? She thought again of herself and her husband and the woman he so strangely loved. He too had said that we live to be happy so short a time and we are so long dead. She pondered long and intently, and suddenly, as summer lightning flashes across the darkness of the night, she made a discovery which filled her with tremulous surprise; for she found that in her heart was no longer anger with her husband nor jealousy of her rival. A notion dawned on some remote horizon of her consciousness and like the morning sun suffused her soul with a tender, blissful glow. Out of the tragedy of that unknown Irishman's death she gathered elatedly the courage for a desperate resolution. Her heart beat quickly, she was impatient to carry it into effect. A passion for self-sacrifice seized her.

The music had stopped, the ball was over; most of the passengers would have gone to bed and the rest would be in the smoking-room. She went down to her cabin and met no one on the way. She took her writing pad and wrote a letter to her husband:

My dear. It is Christmas Day and I want to tell you that my heart is filled with kindly thoughts towards both of you. I have been foolish and unreasonable. I think we should allow those we care for to be happy in their own way, and we should care for them enough not to let it make us unhappy. I want you to know that I grudge you none of the joy that has so strangely come into your life. I am no longer jealous, nor hurt, nor vindictive. Do not think I shall be unhappy or lonely. If ever you feel that you need me, come to me, and I will welcome you with a cheerful spirit and without reproach or ill-will. I am most grateful for all the years of happiness and of tenderness that you gave me, and in return I wish to offer you an affection which makes no claim on you and is, I hope, utterly disinterested. Think kindly of me and be happy, happy, happy.

She signed her name and put the letter into an envelope. Though it would not go till they reached Port Said she wanted to place it at once in the letter-box. When she had done this, beginning to undress, she looked at herself in the glass. Her eyes were shining and under her rouge her colour was bright. The future was no longer desolate, but bright with a fair hope. She slipped into bed and fell at once into a sound and dreamless sleep.

A Casual Affair

I AM telling this story in the first person, though I am in no way connected with it, because I do not want to pretend to the reader that I know more about it than I really do. The facts are as I state them, but the reasons for them I can only guess, and it may be that when the reader has read them he will think me wrong. No one can know for certain. But if you are interested in human nature there are few things more diverting than to consider the motives that have resulted in certain actions. It was only by chance that I heard anything of the unhappy circumstances at all. I was spending two or three days on an island on the north coast of Borneo and the District Officer had very kindly offered to put me up. I had been roughing it for some time and I was glad enough to have a rest. The island had been at one time a place of some consequence, with a Governor of its own, but was so no longer; and now there was nothing much to be seen of its former importance except the imposing stone house in which the Governor had once lived and which now the District Officer, grumblingly because of its unnecessary size, inhabited. But it was a comfortable house to stay in, with an immense drawing-room, a dining-room large enough to seat forty people, and lofty, spacious bedrooms. It was shabby, because the government at Singapore very wisely spent as little money on it as possible; but I rather liked this, and the heavy official furniture gave it a sort of dull stateliness that was amusing. The garden was too large for the District Officer to keep up and it was a wild tangle of tropical vegetation. His name was

Arthur Low; he was a quiet, smallish man in the later thirties, married, with two young children. The Lows had not tried to make themselves at home in this great place, but camped there, like refugees from a stricken area, and looked forward to the time when they would be moved to some other post where they could settle down in surroundings more familiar to them.

I took a fancy to them at once. The D.O. had an easy manner and a humorous way with him. I am sure he performed his various duties admirably, but he did everything he could to avoid the official demeanour. He was slangy of speech and pleasantly caustic. It was charming to see him play with the two children. It was quite obvious that he had found marriage a very satisfactory state. Mrs. Low was an extremely nice little woman, plump, with dark eyes under fine eyebrows, not very pretty, but certainly attractive. She looked healthy and she had high spirits. They chaffed one another continually and each one seemed to look upon the other as immensely comic. Their jokes were neither very good nor very new, but they thought them so killing that you were obliged to laugh with them.

I think they were glad to see me, especially Mrs. Low, for with nothing much to do but keep an eye on the house and the children, she was thrown very much on her own resources. There were so few white people on the island that the social life was soon exhausted; and before I had been there twenty-four hours she pressed me to stay a week, a month or a year. On the evening of my arrival they gave a dinner-party to which the official population, the government surveyor, the doctor, the schoolmaster, the chief of constabulary, were invited, but on the following evening the three of us dined by ourselves. At the dinner-party the guests had brought their house-boys to help, but that night we were waited on by the Lows' one boy and my travelling servant. They brought in the coffee and left us to ourselves. Low and I lit cheroots.

"You know that I've seen you before," said Mrs. Low.

"Where?" I asked.

"In London. At a party. I heard someone point you out to somebody else. In Carlton House Terrace at Lady Kastellan's."

"Oh? When was that?"

"Last time we were home on leave. There were Russian dancers."

"I remember. About two or three years ago. Fancy you being there!"

"That's exactly what we said to one another at the time," said Low, with his slow, engaging smile. "We'd never been at such a party in our lives."

"It made a great splash, you know," I said. "It was *the* party of the season. Did you enjoy it?"

"I hated every minute of it," said Mrs. Low.

"Don't let's overlook the fact that you insisted on going, Bee," said Low. "I knew we'd be out of it among all those swells. My dress clothes were the same I'd had at Cambridge and they'd never been much of a fit."

"I bought a frock specially at Peter Robinson's. It looked lovely in the shop. I wished I hadn't wasted so much money when I got there; I never felt so dowdy in my life."

"Well, it didn't much matter. We weren't introduced to anybody."

I remembered the party quite well. The magnificent rooms in Carlton House Terrace had been decorated with great festoons of yellow roses and at one end of the vast drawing-room a stage had been erected. Special costumes of the Regency period had been designed for the dancers and a modern composer had written the music for the two charming ballets they danced. It was hard to look at it all and not allow the vulgar thought to cross one's mind that the affair must have cost an enormous amount of money. Lady Kastellan was a beautiful woman and a great hostess, but I do not think anyone would have ascribed to her any vast amount of kindliness, she knew too many people to care much for any one in particular, and I couldn't help wondering why she had asked to such a grand party two obscure and quite unimportant little persons from a distant colony.

"Had you known Lady Kastellan long?" I asked.

"We didn't know her at all. She sent us a card and we went because I wanted to see what she was like," said Mrs. Low.

"She's a very able woman," I said.

"I dare say she is. She hadn't an idea who we were when the butler man announced us, but she remembered at once. 'Oh, yes,' she said, 'you're poor Jack's friends. Do go and find yourselves seats where you can see. You'll adore Lifar, he's too marvellous.' And then she turned to say how d'you do to the next people. But she gave me a look. She wondered how much I knew and she saw at once that I knew everything."

"Don't talk such nonsense, darling," said Low. "How could she know all you think she did by just looking at you, and how could you tell what she was thinking?"

"It's true, I tell you. We said everything in that one look, and unless I'm very much mistaken I spoilt her party for her."

Low laughed and I smiled, for Mrs. Low spoke in a tone of triumphant vindictiveness.

"You are terribly indiscreet, Bee."

"Is she a great friend of yours?" Mrs. Low asked me.

"Hardly. I've met her here and there for fifteen years. I've been to a good many parties at her house. She gives very good parties and she always asks you to meet the people you want to see."

"What d'you think of her?"

"She's by way of being a considerable figure in London. She's amusing to talk to and she's nice to look at. She does a lot for art and music. What do *you* think of her?"

"I think she's a bitch," said Mrs. Low, with cheerful but decided frankness.

"That settles her," I said.

"Tell him, Arthur."

Low hesitated for a moment.

"I don't know that I ought to."

"If you don't, I shall."

"Bee's got her knife into her all right," he smiled. "It was rather a bad business really."

He made a perfect smoke-ring and watched it with absorption.

"Go on, Arthur," said Mrs. Low.

"Oh, well. It was before we went home last time. I was D.O. in Selangor and one day they came and told me that a white man was dead in a small town a couple of hours up the river. I didn't know there was a white man living there. I thought I'd better go and see about it, so I got in the launch and went up. I made inquiries when I got there. The police didn't know anything about him except that he'd been living there for a couple of years with a Chinese woman in the bazaar. It was rather a picturesque bazaar, tall houses on each side, with a board walk in between, built on piles on the river-bank, and there were awnings above to keep out the sun. I took a couple of policemen with me and they led me to the house. They sold brass-ware in the shop below and the rooms above were let out. The master of the shop took me up two flights of dark, rickety stairs, foul with every kind of Chinese stench, and called out when we got to the top. The door was opened by a middle-aged Chinese woman and I saw that her face was all bloated with weeping. She didn't say anything, but made way for us to pass. It wasn't much more than a cubby-hole under the roof; there was a small window that looked on the street, but the awning that stretched across it dimmed the light. There wasn't any furniture except a deal table and a kitchen chair with a broken back. On a mat against the wall a dead man was lying. The first thing I did was to have the window opened. The room was so frowsty that I retched, and the strongest smell was the smell of opium. There was a small oil-lamp on the table and a long needle, and of course I knew what they were there for. The pipe had been hidden. The dead man lay on his back with nothing on but a sarong and a dirty singlet. He had long brown hair, going grey, and a short beard. He was a white man all right. I examined him as best I could. I had to judge whether death was due to natural causes. There were no signs of violence. He was nothing but skin and bone. It looked to me as though he might very likely have died of starvation. I asked the man of the shop and the woman a number of questions. The policeman corroborated their statements. It appeared that the man coughed a great deal and brought up blood now and then, and his appearance suggested that he might very well have had T.B. The Chinaman said he'd been a confirmed opium smoker. It all seemed pretty obvious. Fortunately cases of that sort are rare, but they're not unheard-of – the white man who goes under and gradually sinks to the last stage of degradation. It appeared that the Chinese woman had been fond of him. She'd kept him on her own miserable earnings for the last two years. I gave the necessary instructions. Of course I wanted to know who he was. I supposed he'd been a clerk in some English firm or an assistant in an English store at Singapore or Kuala Lumpur. I asked the Chinese woman if he'd left any effects. Considering the destitution in which they'd lived it seemed a rather absurd question, but she went to a shabby suit-case that lay in a corner, opened it and showed me a square parcel about the size of two novels put together wrapped in an old newspaper. I had a look at the suit-case. It contained nothing of any value. I took the parcel."

Low's cheroot had gone out and he leaned over to relight it from one of the candles on the table.

"I opened it. Inside was another wrapping, and on this, in a neat, well-educated writing: To the District Officer, me as it happened, and then the words: please deliver personally to the Viscountess Kastellan, 53 Carlton House Terrace, London, S.W. That was a bit of a surprise. Of course I had to examine the contents. I cut the string and the first thing I found was a gold and platinum cigarette case. As you can imagine I was mystified. From all I'd heard the pair of them, the dead man and the Chinese woman, had scarcely enough to eat, and the cigarette-case looked as if it had cost a packet. Besides the cigarette-case there was nothing but a bundle of letters. There were no envelopes. They were in the same neat writing as the directions and they were signed with the initial J. There were forty or fifty of them. I couldn't read them all there, but a rapid glance showed me that they were a man's love letters to a woman. I sent for the Chinese woman to ask her the name of the dead man. Either she didn't know or wouldn't tell me. I gave orders that he should be buried and got back into the launch to go home. I told Bee."

He gave her his sweet little smile.

"I had to be rather firm with Arthur," she said. "At first he wouldn't let me read the letters, but of course I wasn't going to put up with any nonsense like that."

"It was none of our business."

"You had to find out the name if you could."

"And where exactly did you come in?"

"Oh, don't be so silly," she laughed. "I should have gone mad if you hadn't let me read them."

"And did you find out his name?" I asked.

"No."

"Was there no address?"

"Yes, there was, and a very unexpected one. Most

of the letters were written on Foreign Office paper."

"That was funny."

"I didn't quite know what to do. I had half a mind to write to the Viscountess Kastellan and explain the circumstances, but I didn't know what trouble I might be starting; the directions were to deliver the parcel to her personally, so I wrapped everything up again and put it in the safe. We were going home on leave in the spring and I thought the best thing was to leave everything over till then. The letters were by way of being rather compromising."

"To put it mildly," giggled Mrs. Low. "The truth is they gave the whole show away."

"I don't think we need go into that," said Low.

A slight altercation ensued; but I think on his part it was more for form's sake, since he must have known that his desire to preserve an official discretion stood small chance against his wife's determination to tell me everything. She had a down on Lady Kastellan and didn't care what she said about her. Her sympathies were with the man. Low did his best to tone down her rash assertions. He corrected her exaggerations. He told her that she'd let her imagination run away with her and had read into the letters more than was there. She would have done it. They'd evidently made a deep impression on her, and from her vivid account and Low's interruptions I gained a fairly coherent impression of them. It was plain for one thing that they were very moving.

"I can't tell you how it revolted me, the way Bee gloated over them," said Low.

"They were the most wonderful letters I've ever read. You never wrote letters like that to me."

"What a damned fool you would have thought me if I had," he grinned.

She gave him a charming, affectionate smile.

"I suppose I should, and yet, God knows I was crazy about you, and I'm damned if I know why."

The story emerged clearly enough. The writer, the mysterious J, presumably a clerk in the Foreign Office, had fallen in love with Lady Kastellan and she with him. They had become lovers and the early letters were passionately lyrical. They were happy. They expected their love to last for ever. He wrote to her immediately after he had left her and told her how much he adored her and how much she meant to him. She was never for a moment absent from his thoughts. It looked as though her infatuation was equal to his, for in one letter he justified himself because she had reproached him for not coming to some place where he knew she would be. He told her what agony it had been to him that a sudden job had prevented him from being with her when he'd so eagerly looked forward to it.

Then came the catastrophe. How it came or why one could only guess. Lord Kastellan learnt the truth. He not merely suspected his wife's infidelity, he had proofs of it. There was a fearful scene between them, she left him and went to her father's. Lord Kastellan announced his intention of divorcing her. The letters changed in character. J. wrote at once asking to see Lady Kastellan, but she begged him not to come. Her father insisted that they shouldn't meet. J. was distressed at her unhappiness and dismayed by the trouble he had brought upon her, and he was deeply sympathetic because of what she was enduring at home, for her father and mother were furious; but at the same time it was plain that he was relieved that the crisis had come. Nothing mattered except that they loved one another. He said he hated Kastellan. Let him bring his action. The sooner they could get married the better. The correspondence was one-sided, there were no letters from her, and one had to guess from his replies what she said in them. She was obviously frightened out of her wits and nothing that he could say helped. Of course he would have to leave the Foreign Office. He assured her that this meant nothing to him. He could get a job somewhere, in the colonies, where he would earn much more money. He was sure he could make her happy. Naturally there would be a scandal, but it would be forgotten, and away from England people would not bother. He besought her to have courage. Then it looked as though she had written somewhat peevishly. She hated being divorced, Kastellan refused to take the blame on himself and be made respondent, she did not want to leave London, it was her whole life, and bury herself in some God-forsaken place on the other side of nowhere. He answered unhappily. He said he would do anything she wanted. He implored her not to love him less and he was tortured by the thought that this disaster had changed her feelings for him. She reproached him for the mess they had got into; he did not try to defend himself; he was prepared to admit that he alone was to blame. Then it appeared that pressure was being brought to bear on Kastellan from some high quarter and there was even yet a chance that something might be arranged. Whatever she wrote made J., the unknown J., desperate. His letter was almost incoherent. He begged her again to see him, he implored her to have strength, he repeated that she meant everything in the world to him, he was frightened that she would let people influence her, he asked her to burn her boats behind her and bolt with him to Paris. He was frantic. Then it seemed that for some days she did not write to him. He could not understand. He did not know if she was receiving his letters. He was in an agony. The blow fell. She must have written to say that if he would resign from the Foreign Office and leave England her husband was prepared to take her back. His answer was broken-hearted.

"He never saw through her for a moment," said Mrs. Low.

"What was there to see through?" I asked.

"Don't you know what she wrote to him? I do."

"Don't be such an ass, Bee. You can't possibly know."

"Ass yourself. Of course I do. She put it up to him. She threw herself on his mercy. She dragged in her father and mother. She brought in her children; I bet that was the first thought she'd given them since they were born. She knew that he loved her so much that he was willing to do everything in the world for her, even lose her. She knew that he was prepared to accept the sacrifice of his love, his life, his career, everything for her sake, and she let him make it. She let the offer come from him. She let him persuade her to accept it."

I listened to Mrs. Low with a smile, but with attention. She was a woman and she felt instinctively how a woman in those circumstances would act. She thought it hateful, but she felt in her bones that in just that way would she herself have acted. Of course it was pure invention, with nothing but J.'s letter as a foundation, but I had an impression that it was very likely.

That was the last letter in the bundle.

I was astonished. I had known Lady Kastellan for a good many years, but only casually; and I knew her husband even less. He was immersed in politics, he was Under-Secretary at the Home Office at the time of the great do to which the Lows and I had been invited; and I never saw him but in his own house. Lady Kastellan had the reputation of being a beauty; she was tall and her figure was good in a massive way. She had a lovely skin. Her blue eyes were large, set rather wide apart and her face was broad. It gave her a slightly cow-like look. She had pretty pale brown hair and she held herself superbly. She was a woman of great self-possession, and it amazed me to learn that she had ever surrendered to such passion as the letters suggested. She was ambitious and there was no doubt that she was very useful to Kastellan in his political life. I should have thought her incapable of indiscretion. Searching my memory I seemed to remember hearing years before that the Kastellans were not getting on very well, but I had never heard any details, and whenever I saw them it looked as though they were on very good terms with one another. Kastellan was a big, red-faced fellow with sleek black hair, jovial and loud-voiced, but with little shrewd eyes that watched and noted. He was industrious, an effective speaker, but a trifle pompous. He was a little too conscious of his own importance. He did not let you forget that he had rank and wealth. He was inclined to be patronising with people of less consequence than himself.

I could well believe that when he discovered that his wife was having an affair with a junior clerk in the Foreign Office there was a devil of a row. Lady Kastellan's father had been for many years permanent Under-Secretary for Foreign Affairs and it would have been more than usually embarrassing for his daughter to be divorced on account of one of his subordinates. For all I knew Kastellan was in love with his wife and he may have been teased by a very natural jealousy. But he was a proud man, deficient in humour. He feared ridicule. The rôle of the deceived husband is difficult to play with dignity. I do not suppose he wanted a scandal that might well jeopardise his political future. It may be that Lady Kastellan's advisers threatened to defend the case and the prospect of washing dirty linen in public horrified him. It is likely enough that pressure was brought to bear on him and the solution to forgive and take his wife back if her lover were definitely eliminated may have seemed the best to adopt. I have no doubt Lady Kastellan promised everything she was asked.

She must have had a bad fright. I didn't take such a severe view of her conduct as Mrs. Low. She was very young; she was not more than thirty-five now. Who could tell by what accident she had become J.'s mistress?

I suspect that love had caught her unawares and that she was in the middle of an affair almost before she knew what she was about. She must always have been a cold, self-possessed woman, but it is just with people like that that nature at times plays strange tricks. I am prepared to believe that she lost her head completely. There is no means of knowing how Kastellan discovered what was going on, but the fact that she kept her lover's letters shows that she was too much in love to be prudent. Arthur Low had mentioned that it was strange to find in the dead man's possession his letters and not hers; but that seemed to me easily explainable. At the time of the catastrophe they were doubtless given back to him in exchange for hers. He very naturally kept them. Reading them again he could relive the love that meant everything in the world to him.

I didn't suppose that Lady Kastellan, devoured by passion, could ever have considered what would happen if she were found out. When the blow fell it is not strange that she was scared out of her wits. She may not have had more to do with her children than most women who live the sort of life she lived, but she may for all that not have wanted to lose them. I did not even know whether she had ever cared for her husband, but from what I knew of her I guessed that she was not indifferent to his name and wealth. The future must have looked pretty grim. She was losing everything, the grand house in Carlton House Terrace, the position, the security; her father could give her no money and her lover had still to find a job. It may not have been heroic that she should yield to the entreaties of her family, but it was comprehensible.

While I was thinking all this Arthur Low went on with his story.

"I didn't quite know how to set about getting in touch with Lady Kastellan," he said. "It was awkward not knowing the chap's name. However, when we got home I wrote to her. I explained who I was and said that I'd been asked to give her some letters and a gold and platinum cigarette-case by a man who'd recently died in my district. I said I'd been asked to deliver them to her in person. I thought perhaps she wouldn't answer at all or else communicate with me through a solicitor. But she answered all right. She made an appointment for me to come to Carlton House Terrace at twelve one morning. Of course it was stupid of me, but when finally I stood on the doorstep and rang the bell I was quite nervous. The door was opened by a butler. I said I had an appointment with Lady Kastellan. A footman took my hat and coat. I was led upstairs to an enormous drawing-room.

" 'I'll tell her ladyship you're here, sir,' the butler said.

"He left me and I sat on the edge of a chair and looked round. There were huge pictures on the walls, portraits you know, I don't know who they were by, Reynolds I should think and Romney, and there was a lot of Oriental china, and gilded consoles and mirrors. It was all terribly grand and it made me feel very shabby and insignificant. My suit smelt of camphor and it was baggy at the knees. My tie felt a bit loud. The butler came in again and asked me to go with him. He opened another door from the one I'd come in by and I found myself in a further room, not so large as the drawing-room, but large all the same and very grand too. A lady was standing by the fireplace. She looked at me as I came in and bowed slightly. I felt frightfully awkward as I walked along the whole length of the room and I was afraid of stumbling over the furniture. I can only hope I didn't look such a fool as I felt. She didn't ask me to sit down.

" 'I understand you have some things that you wish to deliver to me personally,' she said. 'It's very good of you to bother.'

"She didn't smile. She seemed perfectly self-possessed, but I had a notion that she was sizing me up. To tell you the truth it put my back up. I didn't much fancy being treated as if I were a chauffeur applying for a situation.

" 'Please don't mention it,' I said, rather stiffly. 'It's all in the day's work.'

" 'Have you got the things with you?' she asked.

"I didn't answer, but I opened the dispatch-case I'd brought with me and took out the letters. I handed them to her. She accepted them without a word. She gave them a glance. She was very much made up, but I swear she went white underneath. The expression of her face didn't change. I looked at her hands. They were trembling a little. Then she seemed to pull herself together.

" 'Oh, I'm so sorry,' she said. 'Won't you sit down?'

"I took a chair. For a moment she didn't seem to know quite what to do. She held the letters in her hand. I, knowing what they were, wondered what she felt. She didn't give much away. There was a desk beside the chimney-piece and she opened a drawer and put them in. Then she sat down opposite me and asked me to have a cigarette. I handed her the cigarette-case. I'd had it in my breast pocket.

" 'I was asked to give you this too,' I said.

"She took it and looked at it. For a moment she didn't speak and I waited. I didn't quite know if I ought to get up and go.

" 'Did you know Jack well?' she asked suddenly.

" 'I didn't know him at all,' I answered. 'I never saw him until after his death.'

" 'I had no idea he was dead till I got your note,' she said. 'I'd lost sight of him for a long time. Of course he was a very old friend of mine.'

"I wondered if she thought I hadn't read the letters or if she'd forgotten what sort of letters they were.

If the sight of them had given her a shock she had quite got over it by then. She spoke almost casually.

" 'What did he die of in point of fact?' she asked.

" 'Tuberculosis, opium and starvation,' I answered.

" 'How dreadful,' she said.

"But she said it quite conventionally. Whatever she felt she wasn't going to let me see. She was as cool as a cucumber, but I fancied, though it may have been only my fancy, that she was watching me, with all her wits about her, and wondering how much I knew. I think she'd have given a good deal to be certain of that.

" 'How did you happen to get hold of these things?' she asked me.

" 'I took possession of his effects after his death,' I explained. 'They were done up in a parcel and I was directed to give them to you.'

" 'Was there any need to undo the parcel?'

"I wish I could tell you what frigid insolence she managed to get into the question. It made me go white and I hadn't any make-up on to hide it. I answered that I thought it my duty to find out if I could who the dead man was. I should have liked to be able to communicate with his relations.

" 'I see,' she said.

"She looked at me as though that were the end of the interview and she expected me to get up and take myself off. But I didn't. I thought I'd like to get a bit of my own back. I told her how I'd been sent for and how I'd found him. I described the whole thing and I told her how, as far as I knew, there'd been no one at the end to take pity on him but a Chinese woman. Suddenly the door was opened and we both looked round. A big, middle-aged man came in and stopped when he saw me.

" 'I beg your pardon,' he said, 'I didn't know you were busy.'

" 'Come in,' she said, and when he had approached, 'This is Mr. Low. My husband.'

"Lord Kastellan gave me a nod.

" 'I just wanted to ask you,' he began, and then he stopped.

"His eyes had caught the cigarette-case that was still resting on Lady Kastellan's open hand. I don't know if she saw the look of inquiry in his eyes. She gave him a friendly little smile. She was quite amazingly mistress of herself.

" 'Mr. Low comes from the Federated Malay States. Poor Jack Almond's dead and he's left me his cigarette-case.'

" 'Really?' said Lord Kastellan. 'When did he die?'

" 'About six months ago,' I said.

"Lady Kastellan got up.

" 'Well, I won't keep you any longer. I dare say you're busy. Thank you so much for carrying out Jack's request.'

" 'Things are pretty bad just now in the F.M.S. if all I hear is true,' said Lord Kastellan.

"I shook hands with them both and Lady Kastellan rang a bell.

" 'Are you staying in London?' she asked, as I was going. 'I wonder if you'd like to come to a little party I'm giving next week.'

" 'I have my wife with me,' I said.

" 'Oh, how very nice. I'll send you a card.'

"A couple of minutes later I found myself in the street. I was glad to be alone. I'd had a bad shock. As soon as Lady Kastellan mentioned the name I remembered. It was Jack Almond, the wretched bum I'd found dead in the Chinese house, dead of starvation. I'd known him quite well. It never struck me for a moment that it was he. Why, I'd dined and played cards with him, and we'd played tennis together. It was awful to think of him dying quite near me and me never knowing. He must have known he only had to send me a message and I'd have done something. I made my way into St. James's Park and sat down. I wanted to have a good think."

I could understand that it was a shock to Arthur Low to discover who the dead wastrel had been, for it was a shock to me too. Oddly enough I also had known him. Not intimately, but as a man I met at parties and now and then at a house in the country where we were both passing the week-end. Except that it was years since I had even thought of him it would have been stupid of me not to put two and two together. With his name there flashed back into my memory all my recollections of him. So that was why he had suddenly thrown up a career he liked so much! At that time, it was just after the war, I happened to know several people in the Foreign Office; Jack Almond was thought the cleverest of all the young men attached to it, and the highest posts the Diplomatic Service had to offer were within his reach. Of course it meant waiting. But it did seem absurd for him to fling away his chances in order to go into business in the Far East. His friends did all they could to dissuade him. He said he had had losses and found it impossible to live on his salary. One would have thought he could scrape along till things grew better. I remembered very well what he looked like. He was tall and well-made, a trifle dressy, but he was young enough to carry off his faultless clothes with a dash, with dark brown hair, very neat and sleek, blue eyes with very long lashes, and a fresh brilliant colour. He looked the picture of health. He was amusing, gay and quick-witted. I never knew anyone who had more charm. It is a dangerous quality and those who have it trade on it. Often they think it enough to get them through life without any further effort. It is well to be on one's guard against it. But with Jack Almond it was the expression of a sweet and generous nature. He delighted because he was delightful. He was entirely without conceit. He had a gift for languages, he spoke French and German without a trace of accent, and his manners were admirable. You felt that when the time came he would play the part of an ambassador to a foreign power in the grand style. No one could fail to like him. It was not strange that Lady Kastellan should have fallen madly in love with him. My fancy ran away with me. What is there more moving than young love? The walks together of that handsome pair in one of the parks in the warm evenings of early summer, the dances they went to where he held her in his arms, the enchantment of the secret they shared when they exchanged glances across a dinner-table, and the passionate encounters, hurried and dangerous, but worth a thousand risks, when at some clandestine meeting-place they could give themselves to the fulfilment of their desire. They drank the milk of Paradise.

How frightful that the end of it all should have been so tragic!

"How did you know him?" I now asked Low.

"He was with Dexter and Farmilow. You know, the shipping people. He had quite a good job. He'd brought letters to the Governor and people like that. I was in Singapore at the time. I think I met him first at the club. He was damned good at games and all that sort of thing. Played polo. He was a fine tennis-player. You couldn't help liking him."

"Did he drink, or what?"

"No." Arthur Low was quite emphatic. "He was one of the best. The women were crazy about him, and you couldn't blame them. He was one of the most decent fellows I've ever met."

I turned to Mrs. Low.

"Did you know him?"

"Only just. When Arthur and I were married we went to Perak. He was sweet, I remember that. He had the longest eyelashes I've ever seen on a man."

"He was out quite a long time without going home.

Five years, I think. I don't want to use hackneyed phrases, but the fact is I can't say it in any other way, he'd won golden opinions. There were a certain number of fellows who'd been rather sick at his being shoved into a damned good job by influence, but they couldn't deny that he'd made good. We knew about his having been in the F.O. and all that, but he never put on any frills."

"I think what took me," Mrs. Low interrupted, "was that he was so tremendously alive. It bucked you up just to talk to him."

"He had a wonderful send-off when he sailed. I happened to have run up to Singapore for a couple of days and I went to the dinner at the Europe the night before. We all got rather tight. It was a grand lark. There was quite a crowd to see him off. He was only going for six months. I think everybody looked forward to his coming back. It would have been better for him if he never had."

"Why, what happened then?"

"I don't know exactly. I'd been moved again, and I was right away north."

How exasperating! It is really much easier to invent a story out of your own head than to tell one about real people, of whom you not only must guess the motives, but whose behaviour even at crucial moments you are ignorant of.

"He was a very good chap, but he was never an intimate friend of ours, you know how cliquey Singapore is, and he moved in rather more exalted circles than we did; when we went north I forgot about him. But one day at the club I heard a couple of fellows talking. Walton and Kenning. Walton had just come up from Singapore. There'd been a big polo match.

" 'Did Almond play?' asked Kenning.

" 'You bet your life he didn't,' said Walton. 'They kicked him out of the team last season.'

"I interrupted.

" 'What *are* you talking about?' I said.

" 'Don't you know?' said Walton. 'He's gone all to pot, poor devil.'

" 'How?' I asked.

" 'Drink.'

" 'They say he dopes too,' said Kenning.

" 'Yes, I've heard that,' said Walton. 'He won't last long at that rate. Opium, isn't it?'

" 'If he doesn't look out he'll lose his job,' said Kenning.

"I couldn't make it out," Low went on. "He was the last man I should ever have expected to go that way. He was so typically English and he was a gentleman and all that. It appeared that Walton had travelled out with him on the same ship when Jack came back from leave. He joined the ship at Marseilles. He was rather low, but there was nothing funny about that; a lot of people don't feel any too good when they're leaving home and have to get back to the mill. He drank a good deal. Fellows do that sometimes too. But Walton said rather a curious thing about him. He said it looked as if the life had gone out of him. You couldn't help noticing it because he'd always had such high spirits. There'd been a general sort of idea that he was engaged to some girl in England and on the ship they jumped to the conclusion that she'd thrown him over."

"That's what I said when Arthur told me," said Mrs. Low. "After all, five years is a long time to leave a girl."

"Anyhow they thought he'd get over it when he got back to work. But he didn't, unfortunately. He went from bad to worse. A lot of people liked him and they did all they could to persuade him to pull himself together. But there was nothing doing. He just told them to mind their own business. He was snappy and rude, which was funny because he'd always been so nice to everybody. Walton said you could hardly believe it was the same man. Government House dropped him and a lot of others followed suit. Lady Ormonde, the Governor's wife, was a snob, she knew he was well-connected and all that, and she wouldn't have given him the cold shoulder unless things had got pretty bad. He was a nice chap, Jack Almond, it seemed a pity that he should make such a mess of things. I was sorry, you know, but of course it didn't impair my appetite or disturb my night's sleep. A few months later I happened to be in Singapore myself, and when I went to the club I asked about him. He'd lost his job all right, it appeared that he often didn't go to the office for two or three days at a time; and I was told that someone had made him manager of a rubber estate in Sumatra in the hope that away from the temptations of Singapore he might pull himself together. You see, everyone had liked him so much, they couldn't bear the thought of his going under without some sort of a struggle. But it was no good. The opium had got him. He didn't keep the job in Sumatra long and he was back again in Singapore. I heard afterwards that you would hardly have recognised him. He'd always been so spruce and smart; he was shabby and unwashed and wild-eyed. A number of fellows at the club got together and arranged something. They felt they had to give him one more chance and they sent him out to Sarawak. But it wasn't any use. The fact is, I think, he didn't want to be helped. I think he just wanted to go to hell in his own way and be as quick as he could about it. Then he disappeared; someone said he'd gone home; anyhow he was forgotten. You know how people drop out in the F.M.S. I suppose that's why when I found a dead man in a sarong, with a beard, lying in a little smelly room in a Chinese house thirty miles from anywhere, it never occurred to me for a moment that it might be Jack Almond. I hadn't heard his name for years."

"Just think what he must have gone through in that

time," said Mrs. Low, and her eyes were bright with tears, for she had a good and tender heart.

"The whole thing's inexplicable," said Low.

"Why?" I asked.

"Well, if he was going to pieces, why didn't he do it when he first came out? His first five years he was all right. One of the best. If this affair of his had broken him you'd have expected him to break when it was all fresh. All that time he was as gay as a bird. You'd have said he hadn't a care in the world. From all I heard it was a different man who came back from leave."

"Something happened during those six months in London," said Mrs. Low. "That's obvious."

"We shall never know," sighed Low.

"But we can guess," I smiled. "That's where the novelist comes in. Shall I tell you what I think happened?"

"Fire away."

"Well, I think that during those first five years he was buoyed up by the sacrifice he'd made. He had a chivalrous soul. He had given up everything that made life worth living to him to save the woman he loved better than anything in the world. I think he had an exaltation of spirit that never left him. He loved her still, with all his heart; most of us fall in and out of love; some men can only love once, and I think he was one of them. And in a strange way he was happy because he'd been able to sacrifice his happiness for the sake of someone who was worthy of the sacrifice. I think she was always in his thoughts. Then he went home. I think he loved her as much as ever and I don't suppose he ever doubted that her love was as strong and enduring as his. I don't know what he expected. He may have thought she'd see it was no good fighting her inclination any more and would run away with him. It may have been that he'd have been satisfied to realise that she loved him still. It was inevitable that they should meet; they lived in the same world. He saw that she didn't care a row of pins for him any longer. He saw that the passionate girl had become a prudent, experienced woman of the world, he saw that she'd never loved him as he thought she loved him, and he may have suspected that she'd lured him coldly into making the sacrifice that was to save her. He saw her at parties, self-possessed and triumphant. He knew that the lovely qualities he'd ascribed to her were of his own imagining and she was just an ordinary woman who had been carried away by a momentary infatuation and having got over it had returned to her true life. A great name, wealth, social distinction, worldly success: those were the things that mattered to her. He'd sacrificed everything, his friends, his familiar surroundings, his profession, his usefulness in the world, all that gives value to existence – for nothing. He'd been cheated, and it broke him. Your friend Walton said the true thing, you noticed it yourself, he said it looked as if the life had gone out of him. It had. After that he didn't care any more, and perhaps the worst thing was that even with it all, though he knew Lady Kastellan for what she was, he loved her still. I know nothing more shattering than to love with all your heart, than not to be able however hard you try to break yourself of it, someone who you know is worthless. Perhaps that is why he took to opium. To forget and to remember."

It was a long speech I had made, and now I stopped.

"All that's only fancy," said Low.

"I know it is," I answered, "but it seems to fit the circumstances."

"There must have been a weak strain in him. Otherwise he could have fought and conquered."

"Perhaps. Perhaps there is always a certain weakness attached to such great charm as he possessed. Perhaps few people love as wholeheartedly and as devotedly as he loved. Perhaps he didn't want to fight and conquer. I can't bring myself to blame him."

I didn't add, because I was afraid they would think

it cynical, that maybe if only Jack Almond hadn't had those wonderfully long eyelashes he might now have been alive and well, minister to some foreign power and on the high road to the Embassy in Paris.

"Let's go into the drawing-room," said Mrs. Low. "The boy wants to clear the table."

And that was the end of Jack Almond.